D1529051

Deliver Us From Evil

Dee Smith

DELIVER US
from EVIL

DEE SMITH

ISBN: 1-4392-0833-6
ISBN-13: 9781439208335

Visit www.booksurge.com to order additional copies.

ACKNOWLEDGMENTS

God placed into my life some special people who encouraged me. With a heart overflowing with love, Jeannette Clift George, the founder of A.D. Players, a teacher extraordinaire, an amazing actress, and a writer, took time out of her busy schedule to pray with me, review my work, and give me valuable tips. The Vandenworm family, Nico, Kim, and Vanessa, devoted Christian friends, never wavered as believers in my talents and gifts. My prayer partners, warriors for Christ, prayed for my spiritual protection during my research into satanic rituals and cults.

Two written resources had a powerful impact on me, urged me on, and demonstrated the grave need for immediate action by parents, teachers, and all Christians in our troubled age. One is a true story of a teen's descent into drugs and Satanism, culminating in his suicide. Written in his own words by entries in his journal, this young man traced his own journey into tragedy. The other is Marcia Montenegro, a former practitioner of astrology and author of New Age journals, who became a Christian and thereafter founded a web site ministry, CANA (www.christiananswersforthenewage.org.), and authored *Spellbound* (Cook Communications, 2006).

I thank two courageous mothers for sharing stories about their own child seduced into cults through music with messages of suicide, illicit sex, and drugs. Their heartbreaking accounts convinced me I must continue. To secure their privacy, I will not provide the names of these mothers.

Finally, thanks to my editor, Susanne Lakin. Glenn Rambo and Candice Spears of RSWriting Services and FBI Special Agent (Ret.) Paul Hayes provided invaluable information about FBI procedures and practices in child abduction cases, SECI (Southeast European Cooperative Initiative) Operation Mirage 2003 about international child sex trafficking, federal and local criminal justice procedures, and the Federal Witness Protection Program.

Dee Smith
August 2008

Dedicated to the Glory of God

Have nothing to do with the fruitless deeds
Of darkness, but rather expose them.
Ephesians 4:11(NIV)

Chapter 1
Beginnings

The beatings started after he lost his job. Angela recalled that it had happened just before her tenth birthday three years ago. Before that, she had memories of living on a farm with her dad. They were good memories about a pretty house with oak trees in front. That's all she remembered.

Taking advantage of the shade nearby, Angela sat beneath a live oak tree. The blistering August sun softened the asphalt street passing through the town of No Name, a back roads town in Texas. Once a former oil boomtown, No Name wasn't even a dot on the state road maps these days. Born and raised here, Angela knew the odds were against ever leaving, but she had dreams—big dreams.

Until then, she must return to the broken-down shotgun house just over the knoll where she and Pa lived. Her father had lost his steady job and hadn't found another, but as he often reminded her, they had a roof over their heads. She tried hard to be grateful for what she had. In truth, their roof leaked and the plumbing was pre-WWII. She cooked their meals on an antique stove and tried keeping food cooled in an equally antique refrigerator.

As usual at this time of day, her stomach knotted with dread. Sunset was near and supper must be ready, or Pa would get mad. Sighing, she went on her way. *I hope Pa's not home yet. Maybe this time he'll stay out late and I can fix his dinner, eat mine, and go to my room.*

Angela hiked the hill to the cabin, pausing before she went inside. The kitchen light was on and Pa was already home. Before she could scoot by him, he charged out the screen door, grabbed a pigtail, and jerked her inside.

"No, Pa. Please." His fist connected with her stomach, forcing her breath from her lungs. She doubled over in pain. As soon as she caught her breath, she straightened and backed away, shielding herself with her arms.

"You ain't gettin' away this time. I'm going to kick yore skinny a–."

In one motion, he grabbed her arms and spun her around, but she twisted out of his grasp, and his kick missed. He staggered and crashed to the floor. Shouting curses, he tried getting to his feet. Angela scurried to her room, shut the door, and slid a heavy chest in front of it. She looked frantically around for some kind of weapon, but didn't see any heavy objects nearby. Her shaking legs wouldn't hold her any longer. She dropped to the floor, searching for a way to get out of the house. The single window in the room was too high and narrow. There was no escape route.

Angela listened, struggling to quiet her frightened gasps. Relieved, she heard no sounds from the other side of the door. Cautiously, she slid the chest aside, cracked the door, and peeked through. Pa was out cold. He would probably be out for hours.

Pain from Pa's punches throbbed. She tasted salty blood from the cut on her mouth and touched the rapidly swelling skin above her right cheekbone. He hadn't hit her on the face before. Usually, it was the strap on her back and legs or a few kicks. The lower part of her belly hurt where his fist punched her. *Something must have set him off real bad this time.*

"Why me, God?" Angela uttered the question to the empty room, but stopped abruptly. Pa groaned as he regained consciousness. She heard his heavy boots pause outside her door.

She held her breath, shaking and bracing herself for his kicks on her door. The next moment, his footsteps grew fainter as he stumbled to the kitchen and out the back door. She exhaled and breathed normally. He was gone.

She dared not leave her room. Pa may return. Hunger pains reminded her she hadn't eaten anything since an ice cream cone this afternoon. The fear nauseated her and she forgot her hunger.

Why does Pa hate me so? Why don't I remember a mother or sister or grandmother or a family? Could it be—?

Suddenly a memory dropped into her mind just like shards of glass from a broken mirror. Pieced together, she made out images... a blonde woman running into the night, blinding headlights bearing down on the windshield of a car. She had sensations of someone holding her, falling to the wet grass, and then nothing. None of it made sense, yet it terrified her. Sometimes she wasn't sure if it was real or part of a nightmare.

Pa had refused to answer any questions about her mother — or any family. As she grew older, fear of a slap or a kick had driven out her curiosity. Anytime she had asked, his face reddened, he scowled, and told her to quit asking questions or he would smack her. She stopped asking questions.

Angela shifted her gaze to the high narrow window in the opposite wall and watched the sky change from violet shades of dusk to midnight blue. Tonight, glittering stars and a slice of yellow moon shone. Somehow, knowing they shone on every person in every place on her side of the earth comforted her. Someone special may be out there for her. A chorus of frogs gathered at the pond across the field and serenaded her to sleep.

At first, Angela slept fitfully. Throbbing pain awakened her occasionally, but near dawn, she dropped into a sound sleep.

⌘   ⌘   ⌘

Ahead, a neon sign winked *Vacancy*, promising clean sheets, a hot shower, and air-conditioning. Darla French glanced at the illuminated clock on the dashboard. Three a.m. Fatigue and tension caught up with her. The clouds hung low, heavy with a storm. Slowing the car, she pulled off the highway into the motel's covered entry and caught the fresh scent of rain as she exited the car. A gust of wind and large raindrops warned of a serious downpour. She left the motor running and hurried to the entrance, finding the doors locked and the lobby dim and empty. Darla looked around and found a placard instructing the late arrivals to ring the bell for the night clerk.

A sleepy old fellow in a plaid bathrobe tied over striped pajamas unlocked the door, entered her registration information, and pushed a key across the counter. He muttered something and pointed to a row of small cabins opposite the office.

Darla barely got herself and her suitcase inside before the storm broke. Yawning, she switched on the lights, sweeping her eyes over the room. It sure wasn't the Hilton—or even the Holiday Inn—but the bed looked inviting.

Later, a hot shower soothed her aching shoulders. Tension twisted the muscles in her neck and back. She thought the source of her nervous tension must be apprehension. Tomorrow was her planned confrontation with her brother-in-law, George. She hoped for a warmer welcome than the last time they met. She doubted it, but now she was twenty-three years old, more experienced, and emotionally and spiritually stronger than the angry eighteen-year-old who had arrived as rescuer of her sister's child. All she knew was she had to find that child, Angela, and get her away from George. Regardless of the risk,

Darla trusted God to equip her with the strength she needed. She hoped Angela was okay, but intuition said otherwise. She hadn't seen or heard from her niece since the girl was eight. Now she would be thirteen, the threshold of the most exciting days of her life. She deeply regretted giving in to George's threats at their encounter five years ago. She was so naïve then, believing his promises to sober up and take good care of Angela.

Despite exhaustion, the pounding rain, lightning, and thunderclaps kept Darla awake. She wasn't afraid of storms, but there was something unnerving about this one—as if it was a bad omen. God seemed silent now. He hadn't given her a specific plan. Angela's future and her own rested on what happened tomorrow.

Giving up after a few more tosses and turns, Darla switched on the bedside lamp. Because everything in their family went wrong after her sister, Denise, had died in that horrible accident, she must take care of her child now. Her thoughts spun backward eight years.

⌘   ⌘   ⌘

Shortly after Denise's funeral and against her parents' wishes, Darla had walked twelve miles on dusty roads to a little town with an odd name—*No Name*.

Hitching a ride on the deserted farm road had been a hopeless cause—unless the vehicle was a tractor and she didn't mind traveling at a crawl. Walking seemed the better and faster choice. Nevertheless, she had arrived in No Name on that hot summer afternoon many years ago.

Stopping at the first convenient bench she had found, Darla released the stuffed backpack from her shoulders and wiped her forehead with the back of her hand.

"Would you mind if I sat here awhile and cooled off?"

The old fellow already seated there removed his pipe and said, "Yup. Suit yerself, young lady." He replaced the pipe and returned to his newspaper.

Darla sat on the opposite end of the bench, rested her back against it, and looked around. *So this is the little town where Denise lived for five years.*

The pot-holed street, boarded up businesses, and abandoned oil well in a weed-encroached field nearby advertised boomtown gone bust. Main Street consisted of the Volunteer Fire Department, *Bailey's Feed Store*, a one-pump gas station, *Dairy Queen*, and *Bailey Bros., Grocers*, which was the establishment that owned the bench on which she sat. One more establishment—identified by a flashing neon sign as *No Name Bar & Grill*—thrived in the hot August afternoon. A dozen pickups in the graveled parking lot illustrated that.

What am I doing in this godforsaken place anyway? Of course. That poor child Angela, her niece.

Darla couldn't believe Denise was dead. The funeral had seemed like a dream. It all blurred together. The car accident—a young man and young woman dead—a child she didn't know existed. Angela's father—this man with whom Denise ran away at sixteen—had seated himself opposite the family pew during the service. She remembered staring at him through tears. He was a bear of a man— large and angry and wearing a dark suit too small for him….

She cleared her throat and asked the old man, "Is there anyone around here who can tell me where I can find George Ross?"

The man put down his newspaper, stared at her, and removed his pipe. "You know Bull?"

"Who?" Darla said, puzzled.

"That's his nickname 'round here—George Ross's nickname. Don't rightly know where he is, but I'd be willing to bet you'll find him some time or other at the bar down the street." He nodded toward No Name Bar & Grill.

"In fact, I believe that's him coming out right now."

Darla shrugged on her backpack. "Thanks."

She had stopped George as he entered his truck. Even today, years later, she remembered their conversation well:

"What th—" He turned, his dark eyebrows meeting in a frown. Recognition dawned on his features.

"Well, I'll be d—." He stared, open-mouthed. "If it ain't the baby sister of the slut who ran out on me."

"What are you talking about?"

"She deserved to die in that accident for walking out on her husband and child for her lover."

"You're wrong. The man with her wasn't her lover. He was our pastor and had agreed to help us get the child and her away from *you*. The autopsy told the story. It showed she had been beaten recently, severe enough that they were on the way to the hospital when they crashed."

Anger and hate rose in her. She wanted to claw his ugly face. *I can't imagine what Denise ever saw in him—*

"You don't know nothing. Now, get out of my face. If yore here to take my kid get yore butt out of town and leave us alone — now." He turned, climbed in his truck, and started the engine.

Before he pulled out, Darla ran in front of the truck and jumped into the passenger seat, tossing her backpack in the back of the cab.

"I am *not* leaving without Angela. Now, take me to her."

He looked startled, and then cut off the engine. "I'm not taking you anywhere."

She took a deep breath and said a quick prayer for calm. She must set aside her feelings and try to reason with him. Surely, he must love his own child.

"Listen, you can't take care of a five year old without a woman's help—"

"—Don't you worry none. She's being taken care of just fine. I don't need you or your parents to mess around in my business. Now, get out or I'll call the sheriff."

"You don't scare me. The way I hear it you know the sheriff well — from the wrong side of a cell." Darla reached for her backpack and opened the door. As she stepped out, she added, "I'll go, but not far. That child needs help. Your notorious drunken brawls won't look good for you when we file for custody, will they?"

She stepped back and watched him as he gunned the engine and tore out of the parking lot with a screech of tires.

A sense of satisfaction filled her. Just knowing she had his attention was enough. She didn't know why she boasted about filing for custody, but she had planted the thought so he'd worry. She had no intention of turning tail and leaving town. She'd stay and see that Angela received proper care.

Earlier, on her way into town, she had noticed a HELP WANTED sign at Dairy Queen. Setting her lips and squaring her shoulders, Darla had walked toward the restaurant.

⌘ ⌘ ⌘

Meanwhile, Darla shook off the dismal memories about her first encounter with George; however, she smiled as she remembered getting that job at Dairy Queen and sticking around for several years. She had watched out for Angela as best she could.

Darla knelt beside the bed, and prayed:

"I don't know what I'm up against tomorrow, Lord, but with your help, I'll get her out of there somehow. She's old enough now to make her own decisions and she deserves to live in a decent home. Please continue to protect her, God. Amen."

Too wound up to fall asleep naturally, Darla picked up her worn Bible and turned to the Book of Psalms.

⌘　⌘　⌘

That morning after Pa's most recent beating, a ray of sunlight stabbed Angela awake. One eye opened on its own; the other was swollen shut. She tried sitting, but everything hurt too much, and she fell back and moaned.

She stumbled to the bathroom just outside her bedroom door and glanced down the hall to Pa's room. The bed she had carefully made the day before was undisturbed. If he had landed in jail, they probably wouldn't let him out until this afternoon. She cupped her hands and filled them with the rusty stream from the tap. The water's coolness felt soothing to her feverish face.

She patted her face dry and examined the damage in the small, cracked mirror.

"Oh my God. I don't even look human." One side of her face looked like a flesh-colored balloon stretched to the point of explosion. Her mouth and chin reminded her of a distorted reflection in a funhouse trick mirror.

Angela's fear of Pa hardened to icy anger. The eyes that stared back at her were empty and cold. She spoke to her reflection through clenched teeth.

"*Never again* will he hit mc."

Goaded by a sense of urgency, she decided she had to run away *now* or he'd end up killing her. But how? If he caught her, he'd sure enough kill her. She had no defense against his size and strength. Her thoughts raced, and like a gift, a memory surfaced. An idea took shape.

She tended her wounds, hurriedly dressed in shorts and a tee shirt, and limped to her father's room. "I hope it's still there," she said.

Angela searched drawers in the chipped and scratched dresser. As she looked under shirts and sweaters, she replaced them as they were, so Pa wouldn't detect her search. Groping beneath stacks of underwear and socks, she encountered the cool metal nose of the gun and the cardboard box of bullets hidden in the lower drawer. Her heart thumped hard in her chest. "Thank God. He still has it."

She hadn't used a gun, but the weight of it and the feel of the trigger beneath her curled forefinger brought a heady rush of power. It wasn't loaded, but the barrel pointing at Pa's face would stop him. Now she had protection. She lifted it and aimed at the wall behind his bed. Click.

There. That wasn't so hard, was it?

She spun around, looking for the source of those whispered words. Frowning, she tiptoed into the hall, the pistol gripped in her outstretched arms. She heard the loud hammering of her heart as she crept through the shack searching for the whisperer.

Put the bullets in it.

There it is again. Confusion halted her steps. Was she hearing things?

You know, don't you, that you want to kill him?

"No. I just want to stop him." She realized she shouted to an empty room, and shook her head, trying to dislodge the voice.

Thou shalt not murder.

Another voice — different and kinder.

It won't be murder. You must defend yourself.

Angela dropped the gun and spun around. There was no one. She covered her ears. "No. Stop it. I won't listen."

She must be crazy — hearing voices in her head. Finally, Pa had beaten her out of her senses. Angry sobs shook her body for several minutes before she regained control of herself.

"I can't stand another minute here, or I'll die."

Angela picked up the gun and bullets, her mind racing. Her hands shook, but she managed to load the gun and set the safety as she had seen her father do. Except for the weight and gleaming barrel, the weapon looked just like a kid's toy. Loading it wasn't hard at all.

Her plan of escape fell into place. Tomorrow before dawn, she would leave.

Pa returned at dusk. Shaking, pale, and bandaged — no doubt because of another barroom fight — he walked to his room and shut the door. He offered no greeting, apologies, or signs of remorse. If he had spoken a gentle word to her, she might have changed her mind. She couldn't deny she felt some compassion for this wreck of a man. She had faint memories about happier times with him—like his bringing home treats and lifting her in his lap so he could read her favorite books to her.

That was a long time ago.

Angela recalled that one night he had walked in from work so angry he threw things against the wall and kicked a big hole in it. She hadn't understood what was going on then, and she didn't now. Pa never talked about it. He just headed for the bar. Drinking made him mean and angry and she was the nearest target who couldn't fight back. In time, his drinking grew worse and he was drunk more often than sober.

Angela fixed supper and knocked on his bedroom door when it was ready, but there was no response. She set the oven on low and put his plate in. When she finished the dishes, it was too early for bed so she sat on the hollowed-out steps of the back porch, catching some breeze. She looked up at the rising full moon. It looked like a filmy cutout pasted on black velvet and the stars looked as if they had been stitched in with silver thread.

The wind came up, pushing clouds across the moon's face and lifting and dropping strands of her hair. Lightning flashed in the southwestern sky, followed by the growl of thunder. The storms coming off the Gulf of Mexico were swift and vicious, but cooled the unrelenting heat of late August. She had a big day tomorrow— the beginning of a new life.

Angela slept restlessly her last night at home. She had packed everything she needed in her backpack and hid money for bus fare in a zipped pocket. Excitement kept her awake for a while, but she fell into a sound sleep just before dawn. A noise near her bed jerked her awake soon after. Listening but hearing nothing more she turned over to go back to sleep, but what she saw stunned her.

She recognized Pa standing at the foot of her bed. He didn't move or speak, and fear raised the hair on the nape of her neck. She suppressed a scream and feigned sleep, hoping he'd just go away.

Maybe he is sleepwalking.

Angela held her breath, every nerve in her body tensed. Despite her tension, her eyes stayed closed.

Oh no. He wouldn't try to— She sensed by his stealth and heavy breathing that he planned something more than beating her, because it wasn't like him to sneak up on her. She tensed and held back a shudder. His light footsteps approached closer; he sat next to her, moving his face closer.

He whispered, "I've missed you so much, Denise, baby…," and slipped his hand beneath her nightgown—

She exploded into action, pulling the gun from beneath her pillow and scrambling to the opposite side of the bed.

"Get away from me." Her hands shook as she pointed the gun at him.

Surprised, he edged off the bed, fastening his eyes on the barrel of the gun. Everything after that happened in slow motion. She heard the crack of a shot; saw a thin trail of smoke rising from the gun, and Pa's jerk and slow slide to the floor. He hit the floor and was still. *I didn't mean to kill him. Oh, God, what have I done?*

In seconds, Angela's carefully planned escape had disintegrated. In stark terror, she realized she had become a killer. *Why, oh why did I load the gun? I didn't plan to shoot— just scare him away.*

She ran to her closet, stepped around her father's body, threw on some clothes, and grabbed her backpack. Fleeing out of the shack, Angela raced down the road out of town, tossing the gun in the weeds next to the road.

Chapter 2

Deadly Discovery

At the motel earlier that day, Darla had awakened early and was on the road to No Name in an hour. She parked in front of Bailey's Diner, the only café in town. It seemed as if the Bailey family had expanded to the restaurant business, too. Eight years ago, there had been nothing except a vacant lot. She noticed the freshly painted siding, which gave the diner a cozy, inviting look. Elsewhere on No Name's Main Street, there had been little change. Although still in business, Dairy Queen had a neglected appearance. A group of teen-age boys clustered around one of the two cars in the parking lot. They wore baggy khakis riding low on their hips and white T-shirts with symbols painted on the front and back. Their car stereo boomed rap music, causing vibrations throughout her compact sedan and jarring her insides. Placing her hands over her ears, she made a run for the diner's entrance.

Upon opening the diner's door, Darla sniffed the tantalizing aroma of fresh coffee. Hunger pangs reminded her she hadn't eaten since noon the previous day. Because of worry, lack of appetite, and the absence of a restaurant in or near the motel, she had forgotten about eating.

"Howdy," said the red-haired woman behind the counter. "What'll you have?"

After a satisfying breakfast and while she drank her second cup of coffee, Darla asked the waitress a few questions. According to the nametag pinned above the redhead's ample bosom, her name was Marie. The woman was friendly, chatty, and not too busy.

"Do you know a man named George Ross? He and his daughter are supposed to live here — at least they did a few years ago."

Marie's smile disappeared and her eyes narrowed. "Yeah, I know him. Worked here in the kitchen for a while but the boss fired him for drinking on the job. How do *you* know him?"

Darla explained why she was in town.

After checking on her customers, Marie slid into the booth seat and leaned forward as if plotting a conspiracy, her eyes sweeping the room for eavesdroppers.

"That explains a lot of things around here that seemed pretty strange. So, Angela is the girl's name. Few people know anything about her — and you're related to her?"

"Yes. She's about thirteen now."

"Such a pretty, pale thing," said Marie shaking her head in pity. "She rarely shows her face in town. Stays in the broken-down shack where they live most of the time, but sometimes comes to the grocery store for supplies."

Lowering her voice to a whisper, Marie said, "Sam Bailey, the owner, told me the other day that cuts and bruises frequently show up on her arms and legs, but she just hurries in and scurries out, her head down, not saying a word—"

Under her breath, Darla said, "Oh, no. I'm too late."

Marie continued, "Some of us wanted to help her out, but she's as slippery as a bar of wet soap. As a matter of fact, we have a kitty set up to pay for their groceries when George is out of work."

Pausing, her round face brightened. "Say—you're not involved with child welfare somehow, are you? It's about time you people showed up. I always get the runaround the times I called them."

"No, I'm not from child welfare. I'm her aunt and I'm taking her away to live with me. Where does George work now?"

"Nowhere steady that I know of; just odd jobs here and there."

"Could you direct me to their cabin? Perhaps I can find him there."

"It's just over the hill past the junkyard across the street. You won't find him there now." Marie glanced at the wall clock above the door. "He's prob'ly at the bar since it opens about eleven."

The bell jingled. "Gotta go take care of my customer. Good luck—" Marie glanced at the card Darla had handed her and added, "—Darla."

Shaken, Darla sat in her car trying to figure out what to do next. Now, there was no question about the drinking. If he didn't agree or if her niece was too afraid, she would call the authorities and have the State remove her. *On second thought, that takes too long. I may have to take extreme action myself.*

Darla bowed her head and prayed: *Oh Lord, give me wisdom. Please give me the courage and strength to do this. You know what's ahead.*

A surge of quiet energy prepared her for action. In fairness, she should talk to George first—even if she had to find him in a bar. She had never set foot in a bar, but if Jesus could hang out with sinners, prostitutes, and tax collectors, she could certainly walk into a bar and talk to her brother-in-law.

Hesitating at the door, Darla heard a burst of loud male laughter and almost lost her courage. Straightening her shoulders, she stepped inside. Sour smells of stale beer made her want to gag and pinch her nostrils. She held her breath, taking shallow breaths through her mouth when she could hold it no longer.

Gradually, her eyes adjusted to the dim interior and she located George. Ignoring the coarse remarks by the male drinkers at the bar, she walked to him. He didn't turn; he just stared into his glass.

Darla touched him on the shoulder. "I want to talk to you. Will you step outside or sit with me in that booth in the corner?"

George slowly raised his head and looked at her, blinking as if clearing his vision.

"Do you know who I am, George?"

Recognition dawned briefly, and then disappeared. "Look, lady, 'jus go away 'n leave me alone." He turned back to his drink.

Realizing he was too drunk to talk sense, Darla gave up and turned to the bartender, "Look, here's my card with my cell phone number on it. Just call me when he leaves. Tell him Darla, his sister-in-law, wants to talk to him. I'll be ten or fifteen minutes away."

The bartender hesitated, glancing at George, but took the card anyway.

"I don't know, Miss, it don't look like he's going to sober up soon, but I'll call if he does."

Her hands and knees shook on the drive back to the motel. The past hour had finished off shattering her nerves. She had to find Angela and somehow talk to a sobered-up George. First, she must return to the motel and make some phone calls. She needed emergency legal advice and backup law enforcement. Angela must get out of there before it was too late for her.

⌘　⌘　⌘

After eating dinner at a restaurant near the interstate highway, Darla returned to the motel for some reading and an early bedtime.

She jolted awake from a deep sleep. After recovering from a few seconds of confusion, she wondered what had caused the abrupt awakening. She looked at the illuminated dial on the digital clock. Four a.m. *Something's wrong. Did I hear a loud noise? Did I have a nightmare? If it was a nightmare, I don't remember any of it.*

She desperately needed sleep. The events over the last two days had left little time for rest.

Darla closed her eyes and tried sleeping but the edgy feeling kept her awake. Something was terribly wrong, and it had something to do with Angela. She dressed, grabbed her keys, and took off.

Fifteen minutes later, Darla reached the edge of town. Driving slowly, her heart caught in her throat at the scene.

"Oh no."

Red and blue flashing lights lit the pre-dawn sky, and squad cars blocked the road at both ends of town. Figures disappeared over the crest of a low hill across from Bailey's Diner. She parked in the Dairy Queen lot, which was before the roadblock, and ran toward the hill. Passing a group of bystanders, she heard murmuring: "Somebody's been shot." She ran faster. Between gulps for air, Darla pleaded, "Oh, God; Oh, God. Let it not be Angela. Let me get there before it's too late."

Miraculously slipping past the officers taping off the crime scene, she rushed into the shack. Terror froze her vocal cords, preventing her from calling out for Angela. She searched every room of the cabin, but there was no sign of anyone inside. She searched again, advancing further into each room. When she stepped into the last room, she bit back a scream, stepping slowly backwards. George lay motionless in a pool of blood. Uncertain whether he was dead or alive, but fainthearted about touching him, Darla continued backing out the door. Where was Angela? She had to get out of there. Suddenly, a flashlight beam blinded her. She barely made out a uniformed figure holding the flashlight.

A brusque voice behind her shouted, "Stop. Don't move. Now, turn around slowly and put your hands on top of your head."

Terror tunneled her vision when she felt rough hands jerk her arms behind her and cuff her wrists.

Chapter 3
The Runaway

The Greyhound idled in the parking lot of an all-night diner. Angela wasn't sure how far she ran, but not until she reached the well-lit water tower of Sealy did she feel safe. Taking no time to think things out, she bought a ticket to wherever the bus ended its trip. Approaching the bus, Angela saw a placard in the windshield noting its destination as Houston. It wasn't far enough for her, but she didn't have enough money for a town farther away.

The ride was short, but by the time the bus arrived in Houston, Angela's heartbeat had resumed its normal pace and her knees had steadied. She stepped off the bus and scanned the terminal's waiting room. It was early morning, but many workers and travelers filled the room. Deciding there were too many people in there, she walked in the direction of the cloud-covered skyscrapers and ducked into a dim alley. Immediately, she felt pain in her shoulders and yelped as someone ripped off her backpack. There was a blow to the back of her knees and she fell to the pavement—hard! Before she could process what happened, two boys about ten or eleven ran past her, one holding her backpack by its strap.

Despairing, she sat on the ground and bawled. *Now I have nothing. What will I do?* After awhile, sympathetic passersby noticed her distress and offered help, but she scrambled to her feet, brushed the dirt from her knees and clothes, and mumbled, "No—I'm okay. I don't need any help."

A brilliant flash and an ear-splitting boom introduced a thunderstorm and people scattered. Next, a cold downpour and pebble-sized hail pelted the pavement. Pedestrians ran for cover. Angela, soaked within a few minutes, ran toward a major street with cars crawling through the rapidly flooding intersection. She found shelter under a freeway bridge and looked around for a safe place protected from the rain. A grove of trees covering a picnic table, barbecue grill, and trash barrel in a small park caught her eyes. She made a run for them. The ancient oaks sheltered her somewhat, so she sat beneath one on the bench of a picnic table.

Hugging herself for warmth, she wondered what to do next. She had no money, no change of clothes, no one who cared. Self-pity climbed aboard with her feelings of fright and desperation. Would the Sheriff find her and put her in jail? Unbelievably, everything had happened less than twenty-four hours ago. Looking up through the dripping leaves, she prayed the best she knew how.

"Hello. Could you use a blanket?"

Startled, Angela turned toward the voice, which came from the underbrush. As her eyes adjusted to the dark, she made out an old woman peering from a makeshift tent. All she could detect about her appearance were a toothy smile and a coronet of wooly white hair around her dark face.

"C'mon in," she said, beckoning a thin, twisted finger. "I just want to help you. You look awful cold and wet."

Glancing at her crude shelter she said, "I know it ain't much, but at least it's dry."

Angela decided the old woman seemed harmless and moved closer. The woman suggested she remove her shirt and jeans and spread them out to dry inside the tent. She obliged, and her hostess handed her a worn blanket, which she wrapped around herself. Hungrier than she realized, she snatched the half-can of pork and beans and a bread heel offered and wolfed them down. When finished, she squatted beside the old woman and gulped down some lukewarm Coke.

While Angela ate and drank, her companion waited in silence. When she finished and hugged the blanket tighter around her, the woman urged her further inside the roomy tent.

"Why don't you tell me how a pretty, young gal ended up here? Where's your home — you're a runaway, aren't you?"

Angela tensed. Would the old woman turn her in? She seemed kind — anyhow, she was lost, it was dark and raining, and she was on the run. She couldn't think straight and had no place to go.

Nodding, she pleaded, "Don't turn me in. I can't go back—I'll find a job and camp out with you until I can get my own place."

"Look at me." The woman gestured at her surroundings. "Do you think anyone would listen to me?" Oh no, I don't have nothing to do with anybody. I been living on the streets for near thirty years now. By the way, they call me Cora."

Wary, she mumbled, "Angela."

"Come on," Cora coaxed. "Can't you tell me a little bit about yourself—your folks, your home town, why you ran away?"

If she only knew. Angela had an odd feeling of waking up any minute and finding herself in her own bed, with its thin, lumpy mattress and broken springs, the dirty window and water-stained wallpaper. Those objects were more real than her present surroundings.

She jumped when Cora spoke, bringing her to the present.

"I bet your mama is worried about you no matter what happened, honey." Cora gently massaged Angela's clenched hands. Tears filled in the old woman's dark eyes. "I had a girl like you once—"

Angela snatched her hands away. "I don't have a mom. There's no one, don't you understand? I don't have a pa—anymore." Her breath caught in her throat.

Cora's questions persisted. "Don't you have any relatives or friends you could go to? What about your grandparents? Folks from your mother's side of the family?"

Not trusting herself to stay calm, Angela merely shook her head to each question. As far as she knew, there was no one. Pa had no brothers or sisters and his parents were dead. Once in awhile she heard rumors that her mother had run out on her and Pa; other rumors said she was dead. Anyway, she stayed away from the townsfolk, she mostly kept to herself, and nobody bothered her. She was too ashamed of how she and Pa lived.

Angela swallowed hard and tears brimmed in her eyes. Her heart twisted with loneliness. Fright, fatigue and shock finally caught up with her, and the sobs billowed up from the depths of her soul. Her body shook and she covered her face with both hands.

Cora, alarmed, put her arms around the girl murmuring, "It's okay…it's okay. Let it all out, baby girl."

After awhile Angela quieted, sniffed, and wiped her nose with a tissue Cora handed her.

Cora shook her head. "Whatever you ran away from, you had your reasons and you need rest. I won't ask any more questions. Tomorrow we'll think of something. How's that?"

Angela managed a miserable nod and adjusted the blanket tighter.

Cora dug around in the packed trash bag attached to her grocery cart and fished out a bundle of rags, shaping them into a pillow. She handed the bundle to Angela and patted the blanket spread out near the tent. "Why don't you just lie down out here since it's stopped raining? I'll keep an eye open should anyone pass this way."

Angela rested her head on the rags. She tried to sleep but her mind spun with anxiety. She looked at the sky through the trees, searching the stars. The storm had passed, leaving a clear night. Only the brightest stars were visible through the neon glow of the city lights. Gazing at them, she felt a stab of homesickness for the billions of brilliant stars in the midnight sky of her hometown.

She turned restlessly, moaning and sobbing as she went through a nightmare. The nightmare continued, replaying her father's face as he collapsed to the floor. The images relentlessly repeated themselves in her mind like a motion picture across a screen. Finally, the nightmares passed and she slept.

⌘   ⌘   ⌘

Early the next morning, Cora told her of a plan that had come to her in the night. There was a person known to most of the homeless as someone who opened her home sometimes for people in need of a safe place to go for a few days. She took in runaways—no questions asked and no contact with the law. Cora sent her off with detailed directions. She hiked due west as Cora had instructed.

Angela didn't know how long she walked. It seemed like at least four or five miles before she reached the end of the park where she found Cora. She hadn't seen a town larger than Sealy, Texas, and she felt swallowed by Houston's skyscrapers. Surely, she had reached the outskirts of the city when the park ended. At the sight of police cars, her heart pumped faster and she hid behind a tree. *Am I walking in circles?* Further ahead, more tall buildings thrust their towers into the cloudy sky. Once again, the sky was overcast and promised more rain.

Throughout the morning, the overcast hovered over the city bringing a drizzle. Her soaked hair clung to her cheeks and neck like chilly fingers. Angela ducked into a parking garage and looked at the sodden piece of paper with Cora's written directions. Maybe she got the directions mixed up.

All around were shops, multi-floored parking garages and twenty-story buildings—no sign of small houses such as Cora described. Squaring her shoulders, she trudged on. By now, her sodden shirt and jeans stuck to her body and legs. She had already removed her waterlogged sandals and walked barefoot.

Staring at the skyscrapers, she had no idea where she was. At that thought, her courage disappeared. Tears coursed down her cheeks.

Through her tears, she looked at the slip of paper again. The numbers blurred as drops splashed from beneath the eaves of doorways. Maybe if she kept walking she'd find a gas station or some kind of shelter until the rain stopped. She walked away from the cluster of skyscrapers and malls. That took her to an area of luxurious high-rises.

As she waited for a light to change, she saw a small frame cottage enclosed by a picket fence. Unbelievably, here in the middle of skyscrapers was a cottage right out of *Grimm's Fairy Tales*. She walked closer, convinced it would disappear into the misty rain like a mirage, but it didn't. She approached the cottage and read the placard in the window. "P. Jones, Psychic. Tarot, Palm and Crystal Readings. Ten Dollars."

Cora hadn't mentioned that her friend was a fortune-teller. What was a picture book little house like this doing in the middle of a city? Angela wasn't sure this was the right place; she thought Cora had directed her to some kind of shelter outside of town—not somebody's home.

Apprehensively, Angela unlatched the gate and walked the cobblestone path bordered by dripping pansies. Taking a deep breath, she rang the doorbell. The door opened, and Angela looked up at a tall woman wearing a colorful printed caftan covering her immense size.

"I've been expecting you. You're the young girl Cora found, aren't you?" Her voice was throaty and rich. Angela felt calmer.

"How did you know?"

She opened the door wider, ignoring her question. "I'm Philomena. Come on in, we'll get you into some dry clothes, put a hot cup of tea in you, and talk some."

Angela stepped inside. She didn't know what to expect, except maybe something like a doctor's office with people waiting to see the psychic. The room was empty. Scented candles cast their glow on polished chairs and a large table. Eventually she heard music—a type she had never heard before—some stringed instrument, soft and slow. She couldn't identify why, but all agitation disappeared and she felt enormously relaxed.

Later, showered and refreshed, she sipped something from a steaming cup that warmed her chilled bones. She felt fuzzy and sleepy, especially as she watched the candlelight gleam on Philomena's golden hoop earrings and listened to her soothing voice. Soon, she fell asleep.

While Angela slept, the big woman reached for the medallion hung around her neck and murmured a low chant. Filmy darkness settled around the sleeping girl, who shivered and tugged the thick robe tighter, but didn't awaken. A smile tipped Philomena's full lips as she switched off the light and walked the narrow hall to her room.

⌘　⌘　⌘

For two days, Angela rested. There was a mystical air of peace in Philomena's little cottage that suited her. She wasn't eager to emerge from her cocoon. But, emerge she must.

The third day, Angela awakened early. Sipping a cup of tea, she stood in the kitchen looking out the small window above the sink. Weak sunlight shone faintly on the bare branches of the trees. She shivered at the bleakness.

Philomena entered, interrupting her thoughts. This morning she wore a matching turban with her yellow, flowered caftan, adding greater height to her colossal body.

"Well, Missy, about time you joined us living folks."

"Oh, I'm sorry. I know I've overstayed my welcome. I'll be packing my stuff and moving on."

"Well now, Miss—Angela, is it—you'll be doing no such thing. Pour yourself another cup of tea from the kettle and sit. We need to talk."

Curious, Angela sat.

Philomena pinned her with a hypnotic stare and muttered, "I've been waiting for you. The spirits in the cards foretold of your coming. You have been chosen—"

"—Chosen?"

Philomena ignored her question and continued, "—chosen for passing my knowledge of the healing arts to you, the choice according to the casting of the bones. There is no mistake."

"W-what are you talking about?" She felt a chill.

Philomena's face flashed impatience, but she explained, "In Jamaica I was taught as a child—much younger than you—the mystical healing arts by my village shaman. The spirits told him at my birth I was a chosen one. Later, my shaman taught me *obeah* and *myal,* which, in my country, are the ancient mystical practices of communing with spirits, casting spells, and calling on magic, spelled m-a-g-i-c-k, which is real—not the tricks of stage magicians. I am now a priestess of those arts."

Angela, shocked, thought, *People really do that? It's nothing but a trick isn't it?* The chill in the room reached deep into her bones. She had an eerie feeling of another presence in the room but there was no one except Philomena and her. Conflicting urges to run away or stay battled within her, yet she remained rooted to the chair.

"I will teach you the mysteries of astrology, the healing powers of plants and herbs, controlling energy forces, astral projection—" Philomena went on.

Reason forced its way into her mind. "No, no you don't understand. I just needed a place to stay until I can get a job and find my own place. I-I have other plans, like saving my money, studying for my high school diploma, making something of myself. I've practically taken care of myself since I was ten."

Angela rushed on, "I can sing and dance, and with a few lessons I can be really good." In her most persuasive voice, she said, "So, you see, I had to come to the city to get my chance."

The room warmed as suddenly as it had chilled. Philomena chuckled in an astonishing mood switch. "Oh, you foolish child. Where do you think you'll get a job? What about school? Where will you live? Who will feed you?"

"Well ... I'll get a job at McDonald's, find a boarding house. I'll think of something. I can take care of myself." Her bluff sounded empty and ridiculous. However, she *will* have her freedom from her hateful past. She just hadn't figured out a way yet.

"There's another matter you haven't thought of, isn't there? You're running from the law and it's not simply running away from a bad home; it's something you don't want the police or anyone to find out."

Angela's heart sank to her toes. "I don't underst—"

"—I have ways of discovering hidden things in the mind. That's what I was born to do. So, you dare to disobey the spirits by resisting their choice?"

Years under the brutal hands of her Pa had worn down her spirit, but not completely. From now on, her life was in her own hands and she must be shrewd. She hadn't forgotten about the horror of the last night with Pa. She was a fugitive and Philomena was clever enough to use that against her. Angela's knees weakened when Philomena's dark eyes caught hers and wouldn't release them.

"N-no, ma'am," she replied. There was a force about this strange woman, and she would be no match against the powers of a voodoo priestess.

⌘　⌘　⌘

Over the next few months, a private tutor, a true believer in Philomena's psychic powers, instructed Angela. Her tutor, carefully picked by Philomena, was a public high school teacher who needed extra income.

Mrs. Meriweather was a seeker of the truth about the powers of the universe, so she claimed. She frequently attended spiritualist meetings, was a devoted student of Yoga, astrology, and reincarnation. Mrs. Meriweather liberally peppered her science, math, and history lessons with each new spiritual truth she had discovered at her last lecture or in a book she had read.

The likeable teacher had a jolly round face, open smile, and twinkling eyes. After awhile, Angela grew accustomed to her unorthodox teaching methods.

Philomena, on the other hand, frightened her more and more with the passing months. The safety Angela had initially felt dwindled under Philomena's incredible mind-reading skills and terrifying trances. The psychic's explosive mood swings flared when Angela resisted learning the dark arts, and often ended with a hard backhand across her face. The hard blows left cuts on her face from the rings Philomena wore on each finger.

Sometimes, lying in bed with tears streaming down her temples into her hair, she prayed to God repeatedly, hoping He existed and heard her. Trapped in abuse again, her hope dimmed.

Her mounting fear and hatred of Philomena fed her determination to run away, but she knew she must plan more carefully this time.

Chapter 4

Stars in Her Eyes

Angela's fourteenth and fifteenth birthdays passed. Her birthday fell on Halloween, the high festival night for witches and sorcerers, and Philomena disappeared for days before and after that day. It was just as well Philomena didn't know her birthday. If so, her guardian would force her attendance at the midnight rituals.

Angela had learned, by observation day after day, some of Philomena's tricks used with her clientele, but her genuine paranormal abilities as a high priestess of voodoo baffled and frightened her. Philomena had abandoned training Angela in the mysteries of the dark arts. In her heart, Angela felt relieved. Fear had haunted her after each eerie demonstration of contact with unseen, powerful forces. One night Angela had collapsed during a séance, disrupting contact with the spirits of the dead, which had stopped everything. Turning on the lights destroyed the tone and mood of the séance, and a few angered clients hurried away without paying. In a few moments, Angela regained consciousness. However, her collapse brought such wrath from Philomena that she had feared for her life.

She recalled Philomena's words and her own sense of helplessness that day.

"You have angered the spirits and you must pay."

Strengthened by pure terror, Angela bolted toward the door, determined to flee anywhere.

"STOP."

She felt an unseen force enter her body and drain her strength. She couldn't speak; she couldn't move.

"Philomena will not call down on you *all* the powers at her command, but you are warned. I will know any scheme that comes into your mind to run away. I will continue feeding, sheltering, and educating you. However, you cannot go anywhere outside of this house without an escort I trust and you will not tell anyone what happened tonight."

The force that had possessed her body, freezing her in her tracks, suddenly released her. Angela dropped to her knees, weeping bitterly.

Thereafter, her bodyguards were either the talkative Mrs. Meriwether or the reticent William, a weight-lifter-sized limousine driver Philomena employed occasionally.

Sometimes, as she rode around the city in the beautiful limo with a uniformed driver, she imagined herself a movie star. The fantasy lessened the pain and fear of her real world and staved off insanity. Despite her fear, a stubborn thread of rebellion kept her spirit uncrushed. Out of range of Philomena's watchful eyes and uncanny ability to read her thoughts, Angela continued scheming about escape.

⌘　⌘　⌘

Staring at her American History textbook, Angela willed herself to read two pages about the "people and events that shaped the American Revolution," her assignment from Mrs. Meriwether, her escort today. However, the woman had left, saying, "I'm going to look over some new books in the religion section. I'll be back later."

Angela shifted on the hard chair and read the opening paragraph for the third time, but a few minutes later, her attention wandered to the large windows overlooking the colorfully designed plaza. She loved the downtown library. It was a place of bright excitement with thousands of books and videos taking her on journeys of imagination. She especially liked the quirky metal sculpture resembling Mickey Mouse at the edge of the plaza. Twice a month, Mrs. Meriwether took her there for the day. They were days with a sense of freedom. On rainy days, she felt cozy and snug in the quiet rooms, but on clear days, she explored the city she now called home.

Today the call was strong. A cool front, trailed by a cloudless and balmy day, had arrived. Nature's final gift before the sizzling tropical summer arrived. From her vantage point, Angela saw the trees tremble with light breezes and gleam in the sunlight.

With a *thwack,* she closed the book. She decided the rest of the day she'd do what *she* wanted. Let Mrs. Meriweather worry for a while.

"Serves her right," she muttered.

Angela returned her borrowed books and hurried outside.

Once outside she spread out her arms and twirled like a dancer. An exhilarating sense of freedom filled her with unparalleled joy. When passersby stared at her, she curbed her enthusiasm and walked sedately toward the skyscrapers.

Sometime later, sipping a Coke, she approached a luxury hotel. She went inside. In the lobby, a large sign on an easel caught her attention. She read:

"CASTING CALL TODAY. **PRIMROSE ROOM, SECOND FLOOR."**

Angela's heartbeat quickened. *Should I go? Nobody will find out. I'll just check it out.*

She loved the singers and dancers she saw on TV and they made it look so easy. After she got away from Philomena, she would move out west, get a job and study singing and dancing. She *knew* she could do it.

Lifting her chin, Angela walked toward the elevators. Within a few minutes, she held a card with a number, had her picture snapped with a digital camera, and the receptionist waved her to one of the chairs lined against the wall. She looked around her. Boys and girls about her age crowded the small room, some reading aloud from a square of folded paper, others checking makeup and hair, and others simply hanging around nervously outside the door.

She heard her number called and her heart fluttered. Her pretense of poise fled when she walked into the room. Three women and two men sat behind a table facing a TV monitor. A camera had been set up directly behind the table. No one looked up when she entered. A light beamed onto a T-shaped mark on the floor about four feet in front of the table. Her escort instructed her to stand on the mark and wait. After that, everything was an embarrassing blur of questions, directions to turn for a profile, and a piece of paper from which she read words she hadn't seen before. Thank goodness, they didn't inspect her teeth, too. She relaxed when one of the women said, "Thank you, you may go now."

Hurrying out of the room, she kept her eyes straight ahead. She felt so humiliated she rushed out the door and took the stairs to the lobby.

Outside, she leaned against the outer wall of the hotel, calming herself before she returned to the library plaza. Soon, her trembling stopped and her cheeks felt cooler.

"Miss, Miss. Wait a minute—I have something to give you."

Angela turned, recognizing a boy from the waiting room.

"Man, I'm glad I caught you. After you left a short, redheaded man came into the waiting room looking for you. He asked me if I knew you—I mean if I knew who he described—and when I said I did he gave me this for you if I found you."

He held out a business card.

Narrowing her eyes, she didn't take the card.

He backed off, his arms raised in a gesture of innocence. "Look, I'm not hitting on you or anything like that. I just wanted to help you get a break. This guy's card says he's a talent agent and manager. If he went to that much trouble, he wants to see you—in fact, he wrote a note on the back of it." He held out the card again.

Deciding he told the truth, Angela accepted the card and thanked him. She watched him return to the lobby. She read the card: *Arnold Peck—Children and Teen Talent Agency* with an address located downtown. Turning the card over, she read his handwritten note:

Please call my office ASAP and set up a meeting with me. I'm interested. Bring your parents. A.P.

Stuffing the card into her pocket, chills of excitement covered her arms. *This might be my break.* Close behind came the thought, *Philomena will never agree to it.* The thought crushed her excitement. *I won't give up—I'll think of a way.* Glancing at her watch, she saw it was almost four o'clock, the time when William arrived. She ran all the way back to the library. She must think of some way to appease Mrs. Meriwether before they went home.

⌘   ⌘   ⌘

Two modern conveniences dwelled in Philomena's household—a television set and a telephone. Even those were vintage items. The TV was an 18-inch black and white model and the phone was an ungainly black instrument. She kept both in a cubbyhole office behind her guest parlor.

One day, her guardian used the limousine for an errand, warning as she walked out, "I'll be back soon. Don't get any fancy ideas while I'm gone, because I'll find out."

It was Angela's first opportunity of avoiding Philomena's watchful eyes, so she went into her office to use the phone. Angela's hand shook as she dialed the number printed on the card handed to her a couple of days ago, kept hidden in her bra. She almost lost her nerve, and planned to hang up, but a female voice answered, "Good morning. The Arnold Peck Agency."

Angela cleared her throat. "Um-may I speak to Mr. Peck, please?"

There was a pause on the other end, so she pushed on. "Mr. Peck sent me a note to call him and set an appointment… I met him at an audition last Thursday afternoon and he gave me his card."

"Just a moment, please." Angela heard bits of conversation when the receptionist covered the mouthpiece. She returned to the line and said, "He just walked in. Hold on and I'll connect you."

Angela snatched another glance behind her, assuring herself no one was in the house.

"Yes. Which young woman are you? There were dozens." He had a British accent and a clipped, rude manner.

She identified herself and his voice became courteous.

"Oh yes. Yes, indeed. Are you and your parents interested? I'll tell my secretary to set up an appointment here at my office right away."

"Do I *have* to bring my parents? You see, I've been on my own for a while now and I can handle anything that comes up. Anyway—my parents are out of the country," she lied.

"Hmmm, that's too bad. It's our policy that we do not sign anyone under eighteen without a parent or guardian present. As I recall, you look quite young. When will your parents return?"

"Er—I'm not sure."

"Well, there's plenty of time. Call me back when they return and we'll talk. I saw a great deal of potential in you."

Reluctantly, she replied, "Yes sir. I understand. Goodbye."

So now, she had herself in a fine fix. First, she lied to the man, and second, Philomena would find out she had sneaked away last week. She *must* have her chance. What could she do?

She replaced the receiver in its cradle and walked toward her bedroom, thinking hard.

Angela had realized as time passed that Philomena's threats to turn her over to the law no longer had any force. Although she had searched the newspapers herself, there was nothing about a murder investigation in her small hometown. She didn't plan to return to find out, but fear kept her with Philomena. She felt trapped by the big woman's spells, curses, and abuse. She still hadn't formed a sound plan to run away. But maybe, just maybe, this will be a chance.

Philomena has been gone a long time. Maybe she was tied up in traffic or something.

"Wait a minute," she said to herself. There was something different in Philomena's office—something important that tweaked her brain, then slipped away. There was just one way to find out. She returned to Philomena's office and looked around the room. It was small, cluttered, and crowded but she was sure something was out of place. She looked at the scarred wooden desk covered with bills, notices, and an unopened envelope from the IRS. The envelope was on top of another pile of envelopes.

"Hmmm. It looks like she left in a hurry. I wonder—" Angela didn't disturb any papers on the desk, but out of curiosity she searched the room. There was something more—she felt it. The room was windowless and lit by a small desk lamp. Objects in the corners were in shadows. There were a couple of file cabinets, a bookcase filled with books for casting spells, witchcraft, and a large volume authored by A. Crowley. None of these items seemed out of order, and she turned to go, dismissing her suspicions as her mind playing tricks on her.

Something else caught her eye. In its usual corner was the safe, but—yes—that was it. The door, usually locked securely, was ajar. She rushed over and looked inside. She almost fell over. Stacks and stacks of neatly packaged hundreds filled it.

A car door slammed. She hastily placed the door as it was and hurried to her room. She was back in her room with a book opened in her lap just as the front door unlocked.

Philomena came directly to her room, but Angela had calmed herself as best she could and hoped she wouldn't notice her agitation.

"Well, girl, I see you managed to stay out of trouble while I was gone—" Philomena peered suspiciously at her. She grabbed Angela's chin and jerked her head upright.

"Ha. Look at me, Girl. You're hiding something, aren't you?"

In spite of herself, Angela cringed, trying to free herself. "N-no, nothing. I'm not hiding anything."

Philomena released her and raised her hand to give her a backhand.

Suddenly, an all-consuming rage filled Angela and she forgot about her fear. Springing forward, she pushed as hard as she could.

Surprised, Philomena stumbled backward. Seeing her advantage, Angela pummeled the woman's chest and clawed her face with her fingernails, drawing blood. Philomena recovered and overpowered her, but amazingly, held her temper and merely pinned her arms behind her.

"All right. Calm down, Missy. What's going on with you? Why did you do such a foolish thing?"

Struggling to free her arms, Angela said, "I'm NOT going to let you treat me this way anymore. You can't control me anymore. I know too much and *you'll* be the one in jail."

"Just what do you mean by that? Do you dare threaten me?"

Calm settled over Angela. The words easily spilled from her lips, her fear quieted. "I mean just what I said. I'm not scared of you anymore. I've watched you and know most of your fortune telling is a trick. I imagine some of your clients would like to know that. I bet some of the herbs and roots you use are nothing but illegal drugs, and the police might want to explore that— maybe stage a raid or watch the people who come in the middle of the night and pass packets to you—"

"Girl, do you realize what kind of trouble you could get yourself into? You're messing with powers beyond your imagination. You could die."

Still empowered and calm, she replied, "Maybe so, but not before I tell."

Philomena glared at her, malice burning from her dark eyes. "You test the dark powers, girl, and I won't help you."

"Oh yes you will. You see, I haven't told you everything I've found out about you." She paused, hoping and praying her plan would work. The idea formed as she spoke, clear and perfect.

She looked directly into Philomena's eyes and said, "There is something that will keep me quiet better than your death threats.

You see, if I have to live like this I don't care if you or your gods or hired criminals kill me. I want to be a singing and dancing star and I finally have a chance—a big chance."

Philomena laughed. "Oh, that fantasy again, huh?"

Angela retrieved the card and held it out. "It's not a fantasy—it's real. An agent wants us to come and talk to him about signing me."

Philomena made a sound of disgust and threw the card down, turning to leave.

In a silky tone, Angela said, "When—not *if*—I make it, there's a lot of money in it for you—legitimate money. You see, until I reach eighteen, I cannot sign a contract without an adult guardian, and that guardian is in charge of whatever income I make until then."

Philomena turned. "Well, well, well, the little orphan is a schemer, too. What if I don't? Your petty little threats don't frighten me either. I could wring your scrawny neck anytime with one hand tied behind my back."

"Like you do to those poor animals in your grotesque rituals? Oh, that's another thing to add to the list of things the authorities may like to know."

In the end, it was the possibility of a lot of money in her complete control that won Philomena over to her side. However, trying to outwit a master manipulator at her own game didn't work as she had planned. Philomena came up with her own bargaining tool. Angela would promise to be a member of the cult by special initiation, sworn to secrecy the rest of her life. Eager to contact the agent, and under a false sense of victory, Angela agreed.

With starry-eyed thoughts on her mind, Angela called The Arnold Peck Agency and scheduled the appointment for the following week.

That night as Angela laid in bed her conscience bothered her. She knew what she had agreed to was wrong, and she had the feeling she had just sold her soul to the devil.

Chapter 5

Transformation

As Angela hoped, Philomena kept her end of the bargain. For days, weeks, months—even years—after the Arnold Peck Agency officially represented her, the truth pushed aside her dreams of instant stardom, and the dreams gathered dust. Grueling and endless acting, voice, and dancing lessons filled her days. Each audition to which A.P. sent her raised her hopes for her big break, but all she heard were the disappointing words, "Thank you very much. We'll let you know if we need you," meaning, "You didn't get the job."

Freeing herself from Philomena's control grew slimmer as each day passed. On the plus side, her training and auditions kept her unavailable for the darker side of her bargain with Philomena. Nevertheless, Philomena stayed close. The woman's hypnotic eyes and supernatural powers kept Angela's will pliable.

What was she doing wrong? She knew she had talent—she just *knew* it. If she could free herself from the merciless control of two people, and just sing, and dance, she'd be happy. Pressure came from all directions. Her homework, acting lessons, and threats from Philomena kept her jumpy and stressed.

Her break arrived on a drizzly, cold January afternoon and her mood matched the weather. Another miserable, hopeless audition—she had thought. The call came from A.P. that evening.

"I just received a call from the casting director at Disney Studios. You and your guardian will fly to Los Angeles Monday morning. They begin filming in a week."

"B-but I don't understand—"

"There is nothing to understand. Just do as you're told. Simply said, you have the lead in their new sitcom."

A.P.'s matter-of-fact, understated manner was his way, Angela realized, but at least he could be human enough to congratulate her. She wouldn't show her elation to Philomena because it made no difference to her whether Angela was happy or not. It was nothing to her, except possible inconvenience to her affairs.

Angela's high spirits flattened. She wanted to shout the good news—but to whom? Deep loneliness emptied her heart, and tears of self-pity rolled down her cheeks. Something good from the past popped in her mind, which brought some comfort.

I will never leave you or forsake you. Angela had heard the words for the first time on a summer afternoon when she was seven. As they leaned against an old oak tree, Darla had read those words aloud from her worn Bible.

Transformation

Darla had entered her life when she was about five. She didn't know who she was—only that she was the nice lady who worked at Dairy Queen. Darla took care of her and protected her from Pa. Two years later, her only encourager and champion had left town without saying goodbye. With that memory, Angela's good feelings evaporated and the pain returned, fresh and new.

⌘ ⌘ ⌘

For two seasons, she played the role in the Disney sitcom. She found out her youthful looks had governed their casting her in the part. All her previous acting lessons seemed useless to her when an acting coach was on the set every day. They dropped her from the show when camera and makeup tricks no longer camouflaged her developing body. Nevertheless, she had fame and a devoted fan base, her replacement hadn't worked out, and the network cancelled the show. A.P. shrewdly resumed her singing and dancing lessons, and, with her enthusiastic cooperation, groomed her for the highly competitive music video industry.

The transition went well, and Angela's career exploded. Promoters and producers, along with her publicity agent, re-named her "Angel." Amused, Angela thought it was a good omen since long ago in her hometown, she had already chosen the name for herself. She said nothing, however.

A year passed, and then another, and her fame and success surpassed her wildest dreams. However, the hectic schedules, psychotic fans, and sleazy, outrageous stories in the fan magazines wore on her. As her fame grew, so did her pain. She sought relief and sleep from prescriptions and alcohol, easy enough in her position for unlimited supplies. In the beginning, it was just a few to calm her before a concert; and then, a sleeping aid after the concert. She thought she kept her drinking well hidden. Before long, she focused obsessively on her single goal, which was sticking it out until she reached twenty-one and gained control of her life and her money.

"After that," she muttered to herself, "I'll move to a desert island, or something just as peaceful." In her heart, she knew she could never give up music. There was one way—if she lost her voice. A stab of guilt pierced her. God wouldn't punish her with that pain, would he? After all, everything she had done since she was thirteen had been wrong and unforgivable. Those thoughts tormented her until a drink fogged her mind and numbed her body.

One afternoon, she arrived early for a conference with A.P., hoping she'd get a few extra minutes of his time. Maybe he'd discuss an early release from her contract. After all, she was eighteen, experienced, and popular with a large following. She was old enough to make her own decisions about her career.

The receptionist was out when she arrived and she walked straight to his office door, which was ajar. She peeked in and saw someone in the chair in front of his desk. Oh—he had a visitor.

Angela backed away, but halted when she heard a familiar voice. His visitor was Philomena. She moved closer and eavesdropped on their conversation.

"I'm here to get some answers," said Philomena. "I know Angela makes more money than what shows on the information you send me. Our original agreement was fifty-fifty from Angela's concert profits."

"I have set up a trust fund," replied A.P., "of which I have full control until Angel reaches twenty-one."

Angela felt the power of Philomena's anger fill the atmosphere.

"What kind of monkey-business are you up to? You know quite well I am her guardian and legally have *control* over her earnings. I always have. You get your commission, which is too much, but I have let it go so far."

Curiosity prompted Angela to move a bit closer in order to see them. The drama and hatred between her two controllers — for a few minutes — drove out her feelings of humiliation.

A.P. stared nonchalantly at the tips of his fingers and said, "Let me assure you, everything I have done is legal and handled by my attorney and in the *best interests of Angel and her career.* There is not much you can do about it now."

Philomena rose from the chair and leaned forward, both hands flat upon the desk. Lapsing into her native dialect, she warned, "If you don' release the money, you be ver' sorry Mr. greedy white man."

Before she turned toward the door, the voodoo priestess hissed a final threat, "Do it soon, so your stupid, sly plans will not burn to ashes and you with them."

Angela hurried to the hall and exited by the stairs.

⌘　　⌘　　⌘

Peck stared at the retreating back of Philomena. Every muscle in her broad shoulders and arms quivered with angry tension. Just a hint of a smile lifted one side of his mouth. "Ah, things are working out just as planned," he murmured.

He had the woman cornered, regardless of her threats. He didn't believe in God or the devil, so her self-proclaimed powers didn't affect him. His own powers were on the realistic side — money, influence in high places, and an underground business that generated millions. He could smell greed, and the aroma surrounded Philomena. She'll be glad to make a deal with him.

He swiveled his chair so he faced the floor-to-ceiling windows framing the Houston skyline. Smoothing his moustache, he thought over his plans.

In a few minutes, A.P. returned his attention to the letters prepared for his signature. He frowned thinking it too bad his star showed signs of tarnish these last two years — her prime years for becoming legendary under his management. The moment he had seen her unusual beauty and self-possession, hc instinctively knew she could mesmerize an audience. Her natural talent took little time to develop and producers and directors noticed her rapidly.

Unfortunately, these days she fell more on the debit than the profit side, and he would not let that happen. It wasn't good business. It was time to put his alternate plan into action.

He placed the signed correspondence in the out box and retrieved his cell phone. Pacing, he waited for his call to London to connect.

"Cecil, I'm delighted to inform you I've put a plan into action that suits your special order. When will you accept delivery?"

Pausing, he responded, "Very good. By the way, this is C.O.D., and I'll deliver it personally in two weeks." He flipped the cell closed, his eyes gleaming with satisfaction and anticipation.

Chapter 6

Jessica and Family

Two weeks before her birthday, fifteen-year-old Jessica Nelson stood at the barrier overlooking the mall skating rink. She had just parted from her friends Pam, Carlos, and Eddie. They had skipped classes to hang out at the mall and meet their boyfriends, Carlos and Eddie. The exchange of text messages laid out the plans. Jess dated a boy already out of school, and her parents hadn't a clue. It only made things more exciting, since they restricted her from going out with older boys. Jess adored breaking rules, especially the ones she considered dumb.

She and Pam had met their boyfriends a football game at the beginning of the fall semester. Jess immediately liked Eddie because he was funny, cute, and wild. Carlos was Pam's choice. Pam—blonde-haired and blue-eyed—had confided that his hot, dark eyes and Alpha-male attitude sent chills up her spine, but made Jess swear she'd never tell anyone.

Jess smiled, remembering Eddie's talent for impersonations. Today it had been the comedian, Jim Carrey. Eddie's looks resembled the star and a few people had even asked for his autograph. If he could fake them out, he'd sign their books. She admired his nerve. One thing bothered her—his swift anger. She just stayed out of his way at those times.

Jess shrugged off the negative thoughts. She had better things to think about—like her birthday. *My sixteenth birthday—me, Jess Nelson. One year closer to moving out and heading for L.A.*

Jess knew her parents considered her a problem child and her twin, Monica, the perfect child. It was fun to humiliate Monica in front of her church youth group sometimes. *Serves her right for constantly trying to convert me.*

Jess turned away from the rail overlooking the skating rink and walked toward the exit. Out of habit, she checked out her reflection in a store window. The extremely different look startled her at first. She had spent her entire allowance on a cut, color, and a radical hairstyle. A short cut tinted burnt-orange had transformed her appearance. Locks of her dark, shoulder-length hair rested in a wastebasket at the beauty salon. Of course, the stylist told her the color was temporary and would eventually wash out. She didn't want to push mom and dad too far. Peering closer into the window, Jess tweaked and arranged the wispy spikes of hair. She brought her shoulder close to the glass to check out the fake ladybug tattoo on her left shoulder. Wow. She nodded at her reflection. She looked great. A few funky outfits and *she'd* look like a star.

Her conscience twitched for a moment. Her dad always puffed with pride when his friends told him how pretty his daughters were—especially their hair. She tossed off the guilt. He'd get over it. Even if he got mad he couldn't stay mad at her very long. She smiled to herself. She was a master at charming her easy-going dad.

She glanced at her watch. "Uh-oh. It's late." She hurried to her short cut at the rear entrance of the mall. She planned to delete any phone messages from the school office before her mom and dad got home from work.

It didn't take long to accomplish her mission—no one was home. She grabbed an apple out of the fruit bowl and went to the family room. Monica sat in an armchair near the patio doors, her open laptop balanced on her knees. Her sister frowned at the computer screen, tucking a dark strand of hair behind her ear. She looked up when Jess took a noisy bite of her apple.

She stared open-mouthed for several seconds and said, "Oh-my-God. I can't *wait* until Mom and Dad see this."

"What?" Jess raised her eyebrows, the picture of innocence. She took another bite of the apple.

"Do you realize how ridiculous you look?"

Jess strolled to the magazine rack. "Ha. A lot you know about what's in, you little nerd." She reached for a *Seventeen* magazine from the rack, took her last bite from the apple and tossed the core into the unlit fireplace. She stretched out on the rug, deliberately turning her back on Monica's smirking face.

In spite of her efforts at nonchalance, Jess's heartbeat quickened when she heard the garage door open. The kitchen door slammed, and her dad hollered, "Hi. Is anybody home?"

"We're in here, Dad," said Jess. She propped herself on her elbows, lowered her head and raised the magazine higher, hoping he wouldn't see her head right away.

Monica closed her laptop, slipped it in its case and settled comfortably in her chair. "Hi Dad," she said.

Eric Nelson, a slender and fit man in his middle years, entered reading the headlines in the evening newspaper. Setting the newspaper down, he fixed himself a drink at the mini-bar. Without turning around he said, "Good. You're both here. I've a big surprise for both of you—"

As he turned, he loosened his necktie. Pausing mid-tug he raised his eyebrows. Removing his glasses, he pinched the bridge of his nose. He peered at his reprobate daughter in disbelief.

Replacing his glasses, he said, "My God, Jessica—what did you do to your beautiful hair?"

The sad look in his brown eyes resurrected Jess's guilty conscience. "Dad, don't look like that—it will grow out in a few weeks. It's just a rinse." She attempted a coaxing smile, hoping her dimple showed. He had once said to her that when they were toddlers her dimple was how he could tell them apart. He sighed, settling himself into the recliner by the fireplace. "Maybe you're right. It's not a tragedy." He thought a moment before he added, "I'm pretty sure your mom won't see it that way."

Jessica thought that now that she had daddy as an ally, she'd take her chances. Changing the subject, she asked, "Daddy, what's the surprise?"

Eric's expression cheered. "For your sixteenth birthday your mom and I plan to give you a grand slam birthday bash—we've rented the grand ballroom at some fancy hotel in downtown Houston—I don't know which one; that's been handled by your mother."

Jess sprang to her feet and planted a big kiss on his bald spot. "Oh, daddy that's awesome. We'll have a great Halloween party—with costumes and everything."

"No," Monica protested, finally rising from her chair and joining them. Jess had forgotten she was in the room.

Monica continued, "—I mean, just a regular party where all of us can dress really nice—no dumb costumes like kids trick-or-treating."

Jess whipped around, facing her sister with narrowed eyes. "Oh yeah—I almost forgot. Celebrating Halloween is against your religion, isn't it?"

Monica's face reddened and she flashed a malicious look at Jess before she turned to her father. "I just thought it would be nice if we did something quieter closer to home—or maybe at the church? You guys work hard and we don't want you to spend a lot of money on us."

"I don't understand, Monica. Mom and I thought you girls would love a big party—especially on your sixteenth birthday.

And don't worry about the money. That's not an issue. You make it sound like we're on the edge of bankruptcy for God's sake."

He turned his attention to Jess. "I agree with Monica on one thing—no Halloween party. This is a birthday party and our birthday gift, so we choose. We've already made arrangements."

"What-ever," Jess said, shrugging her shoulders. She huffed to her place on the floor, sticking out her bottom lip. Turning her back on them, she picked up her magazine.

"Hey, hey, young lady, you'd better drop the attitude," Eric warned.

The front door slammed and keys jingled. *Mom.* Jess's stomach knotted and she ducked her head behind the magazine. *Now comes the hard part.*

Anne Nelson entered, barely glancing at her family until she sat on the sofa, unbuttoned her jacket, and slipped off her high heels. She looked up as she massaged her feet.

She saw Jess and jumped to her feet. "Jessica Anne Nelson, you've gone too far this time." With her hands on her hips, she glared at Jess. A vein pulsed in her left temple.

Scrambling up, Jess planted her feet and stuck out her chin. "What have I done that's so horrible? You act like I committed murder or something."

"Get out of my face and get your behind up to your room." Stiff-armed, Anne pointed to the stairs.

"I'm dressed like the stars—all the popular kids do their hair like this and *their* parents don't scream at them."

"Up those stairs — *now,*" Anne said through clenched teeth.

Jess shook her head and didn't budge, her arms crossed.

Biting her lip, Anne inhaled a deep, shaky breath. She dropped her arm, which she had stopped midway to slap Jess's face.

Eric stepped between them. "All right, you two. Screaming at each other accomplishes nothing."

For a few moments, mother and daughter glared at each other until Anne spoke: "All right, Eric, I'll leave this up to you. Perhaps you can deal with her. I won't." Her anger had noticeably cooled, but she turned on her heel and left the room.

"Daddy, why is she so mean to me?" Jess whined. Easy tears of self-pity brimmed over her lower lashes.

Eric brushed off her attempt to hug him. He placed his hands on her shoulders and looked at her, his expression serious. "Jessica, you are a young lady but you are not an adult. As long as you are under eighteen and live in this house rent-free, you are expected to behave within the rules of this household, which you know very well."

Jess quieted, confused at her father's uncharacteristic sternness.

Eric continued, "Your rebelliousness is ugly and a serious matter. As for this latest incident, you will restore your hair to an appropriate style and color as soon as possible. No allowance until you make the changes. There are no more after-school trips or weekends at the mall for the next two weeks. Is that clear?"

Jess nodded, recognizing she had pushed him too far this time.

Eric released her and returned to his recliner and newspaper. As an afterthought, he addressed Monica, who had said nothing since Anne had entered. "Monica, your mother and I realize that Jessica's bad behavior should not affect the birthday plans we've arranged for both of you. Hopefully, in two weeks your sister will reflect soberly on her attitude and change for the better."

"But Daddy—" Jess said.

"Sh-h-h. It's too late to cancel the hotel. We've reserved the grand ballroom, so there's plenty of room to invite all the friends you want, but no wild ideas or crazy dressing-up by anyone. You and your friends *will* follow hotel rules—posted clearly around the lobby—" Eric added, "You will obey the rules your mother and I give you, too. Guests will be screened and monitored by us and other adults."

He retrieved the remote control and flicked on the evening news broadcast.

On their way out, Monica shot Jess a smug look. Jess felt the urge to jerk out her hair. *You win this round, little sister, but it ain't over until it's over.*

Chapter 7

A Close Call

After they were outside the room, Jess grabbed Monica's arm. "Okay, you tattling little geek, what have you been telling Mom and Dad about me?"

Carefully prying Jess's grip from her arm, Monica continued walking toward the stairs.

"What-*ever* do you mean?"

"I mean the look you gave me when dad grounded me after school and weekends—the smug, 'I-know-something-you-don't-want-me-to-tell' look."

"What's the matter, are you afraid they're going to find out you've been skipping school?"

"Oo-oo-oo, you rat! I'll jerk every hair out of your stupid head!"

Monica left her things at the bottom step and tore upstairs with Jess in hot pursuit.

Monica reached her room seconds before Jess, slammed, and locked the door. Jess banged and shouted. Her frustration increased when she heard Monica's disgusting snorting laughter. In fury, Jess stiffened her arms to her sides and let out an ear-splitting shriek. Whirling, she ran to her room and slammed the door.

Enraged, she flopped onto her bed and assaulted a pillow, shouting, "I *hate* [Thump!] them all! I *hate* [Whop!] this stupid house! I hate this neighborhood, my teachers, and *especially Monica!*"

Jess threw the pillow across the room barely missing a lamp. The lamp teetered dangerously and righted itself. After the red haze in front of her eyes dissipated, her breathing slowed. The throbbing in her head ebbed.

Gritting her teeth, Jess muttered, "I'm leaving this place and not coming back."

She stood, pacing, the room closing in on her. *I can't stand this—I've got to get out of here.* Grounding was a familiar discipline used by her parents, which they could seldom enforce because both of them worked. Sneaking out was nothing for her. She had been doing it for years, had perfected her timing, and had a secret exit.

Jess grabbed her cell phone and speed-dialed Pam's number.

"Pam, meet me at Starbucks near the mall—let's find the guys and do something *fun* tonight. I'm choking in this place!"

Jess raised her window, squeezed through, dropped to the low roof, and shimmied down the runoff drain.

A Close Call

⌘ ⌘ ⌘

Jess and Pam arrived at the same time, and Carlos and Eddie already waited. Right away Pam led Jess out of earshot of their boyfriends. "Jess, do you suppose there'll be alcohol? My parents would positively *annihilate* me if they found out. I've never tried it before."

"Of course there's alcohol, you ninny, but nobody will force it down your throat. It's okay. Don't worry. We're together and we'll look out for each other. Deal?"

Jess was nervous, too, but she was too proud to show it in front of the others. She rationalized that it would all be okay, and, before they knew it, they would be home, nobody the wiser. *It's not as if Carlos and Eddie are strangers,* she reasoned.

"Well ... Okay. It's a deal."

Jess glanced over Pam's shoulder. "Shhh. Here they come."

Once in the parking lot, the four piled in Carlos's SUV, and took off to a country and western club on the northern edge of the county, where they could have some *real* fun, according to the guys.

Carlos promised no ID problems would come up because his brother-in-law owned the club and had let his friends in before. As far as Jess was concerned at that particular moment, the risky plan suited her mood. She wanted to move to some music and feel free. There was a thrilling and adventurous edge to the idea.

Anyway, her family wouldn't miss her because she'd be back in her room before anyone awakened.

The drive took about forty-five minutes. After fifteen minutes on the road, Jess's skin prickled with nervousness. In fact, she was scared. There was nothing but silhouetted pines bordering the road—no signs of civilization. Carlos turned off the two-lane highway onto a narrow, graveled road. Suddenly, every rape and murder of women Jess had heard on the news in the last two weeks flashed through her mind. Consumed with her thoughts, it took her a moment to realize they had arrived.

"Here we are. Let's party," said Carlos.

The thunderous boom of amplified music greeted them before they saw the club—a tin building circled by a dirt parking lot. Part of the building wasn't walled and a cement slab served as a dance floor. Yelling, hooting customers already crowded the building and spilled into the parking lot. The foursome sat at a scarred, beer-stained table near the men's room. Jess and Pam ordered Cokes, and Eddie and Carlos headed to the bar for everyone's drinks.

The noisy crowd and music made any conversation other than shouting impossible. Therefore, they said nothing, and tried ignoring the comments and stares of the men who passed them on their way to the rest room. Several minutes after Eddie and Carlos left, a middle-aged man wearing tight Levis, elaborate boots, and a Stetson shoved back on his head, pushed away from the rail and sauntered toward them.

"I think that old guy's coming over here to ask one of us to dance," shouted Pam. "What do we do now?"

"Just say no," Jess shouted back.

Then she spotted Carlos walking toward them, followed by Eddie. Eddie held two bottled Cokes in each hand, his arms lifted above the jostling crowd. The older man noticed, too, and returned to his place.

Later, a tall Hispanic man approached their table, carrying something in a brown paper bag. Carlos seemed to know the man and met him a few feet away from the table. They had a brief conversation in Spanish. From the corner of her eye, Jess noticed Carlos slip some cash to the man, who retrieved a white packet from his shirt pocket and dropped it into a paper sack holding a fifth of whiskey. He handed the sack to Carlos.

Jess's heart rate went up. For reassurance, she touched the belt-loop of her jeans and became frantic when she didn't find her cell phone clipped to it. Had it fallen to the floor when they came into the bar? She had to find it. Jess caught Pam's eye, and knew from the look on her face she had seen the exchange, too.

When Carlos returned, Jess got up from her chair and grabbed Pam's hand. "Excuse us. We need to find the ladies' room. We'll be back in a minute."

Without waiting, she pulled Pam from her seat, keeping a firm grasp on her hand until they reached the other side of the crowd. Inside the rest room, she went to a basin and washed her hands, signaling Pam to move in close to her.

"Did you see what I just saw," Jess whispered.

"Oh, Jess, what have we gotten ourselves into?" Pam's face clouded, threatening tears.

Jess wanted to cry, too, but that wouldn't help anything. Pam had always looked up to her. Her thoughts jumped from one idea to another.

"Just let me think a minute, Pam. I'll think of something—do you have any money with you? We can call a cab—oh-mi-gosh; do you have your cell? I lost mine somewhere."

Pam shook her head, twisting a paper towel.

Jess said, "I'm beginning to think this was a bad idea. Now we find out we're in the middle of nowhere without our phones!" She moaned, closing her eyes and placing the heels of her hands to her temples.

A few seconds later, she opened her eyes. She had an idea. "Okay. I did bring some emergency cash with me. If everything falls apart, we can call a cab. We'll find a pay phone somewhere. Now, let's go back to the table." She turned to go, and then paused.

"Oh, yeah—let's stay in each other's sight, keep drinking Cokes, and don't accept anything Carlos or anyone else offers you. I've heard about those pills that guys drop into your drink, you pass out, and don't even remember you've been raped."

"Really?" Pam's eyes widened, and then teared up.

Go figure! I'm remembering all of this stuff now. Jess had to admit that her anger earlier that evening had wiped out her common sense.

A Close Call

Eddie made frequent trips to the parking lot, returning happy, high, and talkative as the evening wore on. Hoping she'd at least slow him down, Jess grabbed Eddie's hand and led him to the hot, packed dance floor. *Another bad choice.* Considering the small slab of a dance floor and couples packed in, some swaying in place was all they could do. Talking above the noise was impossible. Jammed close, Eddie's hands roamed over her body in the wrong places, and she felt like she was in the clutches of an octopus. *He's definitely been drinking—or worse.* Jess had never seen Eddie like this. He usually backed off when she set her boundaries, but this was different. Icicles of fear pierced her spine.

Mercifully, the dance ended, but before she had a chance to escape, Eddie pulled her through the crowd toward the parking lot. The harder Jess tried freeing his hands, the tighter he gripped her arm.

"Eddie, stop. You're tearing my arm out of the socket. What's the matter with you?"

"Aw, c'mon Jess. Let's get away from the crowd. We want to be alone, don't we?"

"No! *We* don't want to be alone, Eddie." She hoped her voice didn't show the inner panic she felt. She must get control of this situation.

She tried a reasonable approach. "Eddie, this isn't like you. You've been drinking. Besides, we need to go. Where's Carlos? Pam and I have to get home before our parents get suspicious and call the police."

75

Eddie wasn't listening. He kept reaching for her and Jess kept pushing him away. She looked desperately around the parking lot, and then saw their SUV parked several yards away, the rear window propped open with a cooler resting on the tailgate. Good. Maybe some ice will cool him off and bring him to his senses. Her heart skipped a beat when they got closer. She recognized the source of his abnormal behavior. She hadn't forgotten the little white packet.

"C'mon to the van with me and I'll fix you up with something *real* good. Then, maybe you'll relax a little," said Eddie.

Littered in the area around the cooler were empty beer cans, marijuana butts, and what looked like drug paraphernalia. Laughter drifted from an unlit area of the parking lot, bordered with bushes and trees. As her eyes adjusted, she detected movement—couples stumbling toward the bushes or entwined on the ground near them. With growing urgency, she pried his arm away from her waist.

"What's your problem? I thought we were a couple."

His face darkened and his grip tightened when a thought came to him.

"Oh, I get it—you're a tease! You've been stringing me along. All along you didn't plan to put out!"

He jerked her hard against him, forcing her toward the woods.

"Eddie! Let me go! I'll scream!"

He laughed. "Go ahead. No one will pay attention."

A Close Call

Jess continued struggling, but his arms tightened like steel bands. *Oh, God, please help me. I'll never do anything this stupid again.* Everything became a blur of terror, and when he pushed her to the ground, he fell on top of her and she couldn't breathe, she couldn't move. Gravel bit into her back when she bucked and twisted to get him off. Instinctively, she sucked in air and screamed as loud as she could. Eddie clamped his hand over her mouth, cutting off her screams. He muttered coarse profanities, panting and growling like a beast. With absolute certainty, Jess realized it was too late to stop him now. They were too far away for help. She should just give up.

Suddenly, a calm feeling flowed through her body. Her mind abandoned its confused panicky state, as if another mind controlled it. She remembered a young police officer's advice to her gym class: "When your life is at stake, struggling is the worst thing to do. Remember with rape it's not about sex—it's about power, and fighting excites your attacker."

Jess relaxed for a split second. When she did, Eddie shifted the knee pinning her legs to the ground. Freeing one leg she brought her knee to his crotch as hard as she could, praying her aim was accurate. It was. Air wheezed out of his lungs like a bellows and he doubled up in pain.

Jess wriggled from beneath him and ran toward the building, yelling all the way.

Pam bolted out of the building and caught Jess before she collapsed to the ground.

Jess—I've been looking all over for you. What happened—oh, God, you have blood on your hands! Are you hurt?" A couple of husky men followed Pam.

Sobbing hysterically, Jess pointed to the edge of the woods. "Ohhh, Pam. He tried to rape me." Her sobs dissolved into a wail.

"Should we call 911," asked someone in the crowd.

Still trembling, she answered, "N-no. I'm okay—just some scrapes on my hands and back where he pushed me to the ground. I stopped him before he, he—" More tears streamed over the mascara streaks. "Please, don't call anybody. I just want to clean up and go home. May-maybe a cab?"

An onlooker handed Jess a cup of water and a handkerchief. Pam kept her arms around her friend. Jess quieted and wiped the blood from her gravel-scraped hands. She wiped her drenched eyes, streaking mascara on her cheeks.

Just then, Eddie limped toward them. He saw Jess and the commotion surrounding her and changed his mind. He turned around, stumbling and hopping toward the trees. Two big guys took off. After a brief scuffle, they led him to a pickup, heaving him into the truck bed to sleep it off, she supposed.

After Jess had cleaned up, Carlos showed up. Jess shot a curious look at Pam, who shrugged, implying she didn't know where he'd been.

"Jess, are you hurt," Carlos asked.

She shook her head.

He handed Pam a set of keys. "Take my van and get her out of here. I'll hitch a ride and pick up my keys tomorrow."

Both girls wanted to get home as soon as possible with as little notice as possible; therefore, they accepted Carlos's offer, no questions asked.

The girls were silent on the drive, lost in their own thoughts. Jess's sobbing had subsided once on the road, but she crowded to the corner, still shaking, and stared out the window into the darkness. Occasionally a shudder jolted her body and she would glance fearfully in the back seat as if something—or someone—hid there.

After Pam dropped her off, Jess went to the rear of the darkened house and climbed through the window to her room. Once inside, she switched the lights on and sat in front of her dressing table hiding her face in both hands. Her slumped shoulders shook with sobs and shame. She raised her head and stared at her reflection, feeling as if she had just walked out of a nightmare.

A soft knock on her bedroom door startled her. "Who is it?"

"Jess, it's me, Monica. I just want you to know I'm sorry I acted so mean to you. I haven't told Mom or Dad anything, but I'm worried about you. I saw your light on and heard you crying. Are you okay?"

Jess sighed. "I'm fine, but I don't want to talk about it now. Okay?" That's all Monica needed—hearing the gory details—to mess things up big time. She had to figure things out by herself.

"Okay. Good night."

She shuddered, recalling the horror, and had an uncontrollable urge to take a shower and scrub every square inch of her body even though she got away before he—she couldn't even think what could have happened. Another shudder wracked her body. She hoped she'd never see him again. She wanted no apologies, excuses, or words from him. Eddie was history. She had liked him. She had trusted him. She would not make that mistake again with *any* boy.

Chapter 8

The Prize

Jess had intermittent nightmares the rest of the night. Daylight edged the drapes before she slept without interruption. Awakening several hours later, sunlight washed the room. What had happened last night seemed unreal this morning—a part of her nightmares.

She sat upright, resting against the pillows. Usually, she was up and out of the house twenty minutes after she awakened, especially Saturday morning. There were so many good places for hanging out, especially if she had money left from her allowance. If her parents assigned chores, she wasn't around.

Everything was different today. The narrow escape last night had taken something away from her. She wouldn't trust easily now. She had always believed she could handle herself with boys. Just remembering what Eddie had said about her being a tease and his assumption she would have sex with him eventually warmed her checks with embarrassment.

Jess fingered the gold chain around her neck, wondering what she should do next. She never intended seeing Eddie again. Thank God, he didn't know where she lived, and if he harassed her, she'd change her cell number. Whether Pam wanted to see Carlos again was her business, but she doubted that her friend would. Pam had been scared, too. They both had been lucky. She supposed Monica was suspicious, but she was always suspicious and nosy. Altogether, she concluded that it wouldn't be wise to push her folks too far—especially with the party coming up in two weeks.

She didn't like the rules and choices already made about the party, but there were ways of sparking up the dullest party. She would think of something fun and different. Maybe she could charm dad into buying her that hot red dress she saw at the boutique in the mall.

Her fingers touched the small key at the end of the chain around her neck and she got an idea. The key opened a jewelry box she had hidden in her closet. It was the place she hid her secret treasures. It kept bugging her that she had stashed something very important in there. What was it? She envisioned her opened jewel box, remembering each special item she had placed in it. There was her very first valentine from Daddy when she was five—the one that he had secretly confided she was his favorite girl. Her cheerleading medal and her first ballet slippers were there, too.

"Of course. Why didn't I think of this before? What a great birthday present from me to me."

She leapt out of bed and ran to her closet. Rummaging behind some shoeboxes, she retrieved a locked jewelry box, unclasped the chain, and inserted the key. Smiling, she removed a ticket stub stapled to a 3 by 5 card. Checking the clock, she said, "Good. It's after nine. Maybe somebody's there today."

"Good morning, Arnold Peck Agency."

"Hi, my name is Jessica Nelson, and I won the drawing at Angel's concert last week here in Houston. This was the phone number to call to claim my prize. Who do I talk to about that?"

"You need to talk to Mr. Peck. I'll see if he's here."

A minute later, a man with a British accent identified himself as Arnold Peck. "My secretary said you won some sort of prize. Refresh my memory."

Jessica read the card: "The winner of this drawing is entitled to one evening with Angel as a guest performer at an event of his or her choosing. Please call the number shown below to work out the scheduling details."

"Oh yes. I seem to recall Angel's publicist mentioning something about that to me a few days ago. I'll confer with her publicity staff and will get back to you later this morning. How can I reach you, Miss Nelson?"

She gave her cell number, and then disconnected and tossed the phone onto her bed. Thumbs up, she said, "Yes!" She hoped she could keep it a secret for two weeks. Was it possible the star of TV and film, Angel, would entertain at her birthday party?

"Now *that* will make it a sensational party." She felt her chest tighten with nervous excitement.

Chapter 9

The Birthday Party

Monica gazed out the car window at the flawless sky. Her mother drove, her attention focused on the traffic congestion as they approached downtown. Mother and daughter enjoyed a comfortable silence during the thirty-minute drive from the western suburbs. It wasn't often Monica had alone time with her mom. She was so proud of her mom—struggling through law school and taking care of her girls, too. She knew it hadn't been easy for either of her parents, but they wanted to give their best to them.

Glancing at her mother's perfect profile and dark, curly hair, Monica thought, *I have the prettiest mom in my whole class.* She loved telling her friends that her mother had given up a promising modeling career for her family.

Lowering the window, she savored the cool bite of the air. The lingering aroma of wood smoke delighted her nose. *Perfect weather for the party.*

"Thank you, God," she murmured.

"What?"

Monica reached over and hugged Anne's arm. "Oh, I just thanked God for the perfect weather. Thank *you,* Mom, for thinking of this. It's going to be a great party."

"You're welcome, honey. Thanks for your help with the menu and decorations. I had no idea what teen-agers like to eat at parties." She smiled at Monica. "Oh yes—I thought it was a good idea to reserve a suite for the family so we won't have to drive home so late."

Anne returned her attention to the road, honking at an old pickup loaded with lawn equipment. She whipped around the offending truck and continued, "I'm so sorry something came up and I have to leave for awhile, but I know I can depend on you to check things out in the ballroom."

Monica's stomach knotted.

"Oh, Mom, it's Saturday night and my *birthday.* Can't you skip work this time?"

"Honey, I wish I could—really. But the senior partner at the firm called an emergency staff meeting at six." Anne looked at her watch. "It's five-thirty now, and by the time I get through the traffic and park—God—I almost missed the exit."

The driver behind her leaned on his horn when she cut in front of him. As he passed, he stuck his arm out the window and made an obscene gesture. Monica shut her eyes, but she was a split second too late. Whenever someone made *the sign*, she felt sick to her stomach. Anne didn't seem bothered and merged with the side street traffic.

When they reached the traffic light, she patted Monica's knee. "I'll keep my pager on, so page me if there's a problem. I should be back in an hour. Okay. Here we are."

Monica kissed her mom on the cheek and said, "Don't worry, mom, everything will be fine until you get back." Once her mom was out of sight, she sighed and followed the bellman into the lobby.

Monica checked in and had their luggage placed in their room. She found the ballroom, and caught her breath when she saw the layout. *Perfect, just perfect.*

Linen tablecloths covered circular tables like fresh blankets of snow. Balloons bobbed around easels displaying posters of music and film stars. A small stage faced the freshly polished dance floor. Decorated buffet tables awaited pizzas, hot dogs, hamburgers, tacos and burritos.

She picked up her key card at the front desk, wondering when Jess would show up—*if* she showed up. She wouldn't put it past her, simply as a dramatic demonstration of her objections.

Monica thought about how her sister had changed since they entered high school. She kept hoping Jess would give up her crazy behavior and stop creating chaos before she landed in big trouble. She resented her sister's mocking accusations that she was a hypocrite. Jess criticized all of her friends in the youth group, taunting her that she ought to check out what some did with their time *outside* of church, which would then make her mad, and another battle started.

Early arrivals—most of whom were members of her youth group—came at about eight-thirty. Monica's date, Kevin, waited for her. He was a thin and tall young man who was in Monica's homeroom class. Monica and Kevin were good friends with nothing romantic between them.

After greeting the guests, Monica returned to the table, complaining, "Kevin, I'm so mad at Jess. No one has heard a word from her all day. What's she thinking about, showing up late for her own birthday party?"

Before he answered, she excused herself and rushed to a couple in their early thirties hesitating at the ballroom entry.

"Oh, Pastor Ames," Monica said. "Thanks for coming. I'll take you to your table. Would you like some refreshments?" She led the couple to a table near the stage.

Nine o'clock and the band arrived together. Still no Jess.

"She's an hour late; this is unforgivable. I hate her for doing this to me." *There I go again—losing my temper.* She hated herself when that happened.

"Chill out," soothed Kevin, who stood and gestured toward the dance floor. "They're playing a slow dance. Let's go."

⌘　⌘　⌘

Jess touched up her makeup while her date waited in the hotel lobby. Harry Pringle lived on their block and seemed nice, but dreary—definitely not her type. Harry was in some of her classes but she thought him immature and a nerd because he was on the debating team and in the band. Sometimes in class, he'd stare at her and it made her nervous. He was one of Monica's church friends and she wasn't interested, but he'd pass inspection by her parents. In the spirit of keeping peace with her parents, she had invited some girls in her class who didn't hang out with the top crowd at school.

She didn't invite Pam just to please her mom, because she didn't like her. Jess had better think of a good reason she hadn't invited her best friend. If Pam didn't already know about the party, she'd probably hear about it. The friends hadn't spoken to each other since that horrible night with Eddie and Carlos. Guilt crept into her thoughts, but she dismissed it.

Leaning closer to the mirror, Jess inspected her eye makeup and decided she needed more eyeliner. As she applied the eyeliner, she smiled at her reflection. For the last two weeks, she had busied herself arranging for Angel's appearance without raising Monica's or her parents' suspicions. She patted a dab of powder on her nose, dropped her compact into her bag, and went to the lobby where Harry waited.

When they entered the ballroom, she saw the anger on her sister's face, but played cool and ignored the storm warnings. She urged Harry toward the table and said, "Monica, you remember Harry, don't you? Oh, hi Kevin."

After greetings, Harry pulled out a chair for Jess. She took her seat as if settling on a royal throne.

"Harry, get me a Coke and some tacos. I'm starved," she commanded.

When Harry left, Kevin glanced at the twins, puzzlement written all over his face. The girls glared at each other like a couple of cats with their ears laid back. He cleared his throat and said to Monica, "Excuse me. I'll get another plate for us."

When they were out of earshot, Monica attacked, hissing, "Where have you been?"

Jess turned her back on her, scooting her chair around for a better view of the ballroom entry.

"Jessica, what on earth is wrong with you?" She grabbed her shoulder.

Shrugging off her grip, Jess retorted, "Nothing." She kept her eyes on the ballroom entry doors. She looked at her watch. *Where is she? They said she'd be here no later than—*

"You're too quiet." Monica narrowed her eyes. "That usually means you're up to something."

"What*ever* do you mean?" Jess raised her eyebrows, the picture of innocence.

A waiter approached them. Speaking to Jess he said, "Miss Nelson, your *guests* have arrived."

"What on earth?" Monica hurried after Jess and the waiter. Kevin and Harry spotted the three as they passed the buffet tables and followed them.

Four astonished teens stared at the scene in front of them.

The lobby swarmed with musicians, sound, and light technicians. The area was a tangle of cables, electrical wires, lights, and cameras. Curious hotel guests had gathered, blocking access to the front desk and lobby. An angry man raced from an office behind the front desk and yelled above the din, "Who is in charge here?"

Outside, a chartered bus moved out and a white limousine behind it stopped at the curb. Parking valets ran toward the line of cars snaking into the street. It was a nightmare of noise— hissing buses, honking and shouting.

The chauffeur opened the rear door of the limousine, and a well-dressed, balding man stepped out. He turned and spoke to someone inside. Then the man issued brief instructions to the chauffeur. Nodding, he returned to the driver's seat and drove away.

The man appeared unperturbed by the turmoil around him. His posture and purposeful stride implied authority. As soon as he entered the lobby, the milling crew quieted. After a few quick sentences from him, the upset hotel manager retreated to his office. The tech people moved to the service elevators and the dancers moved to the rear halls.

"Which one of you is— " He retrieved a small notebook from inside his coat pocket and glanced at it. "—Jessica Nelson?"

"I am, s-sir," she squeaked. She hadn't expected all this commotion—and, who was this intimidating man?

He stared at her with chilly eyes. She smoothed her hair and tugged her low-cut gown higher.

"I am Arnold Peck, Angel's manager." He spoke in a clipped and precise fashion. Everything about him unmistakably demanded obedience.

"I would like to speak to you, Miss Nelson—" He looked at the others. "—*alone* to inform you of more details." He stepped aside, outstretching his arm for Jess to accompany him to a corner of the lobby.

⌘　⌘　⌘

Jess returned to their table fifteen minutes later. After Mr. Peck had explained things, she was more excited than ever. Angel's appearance would be electric and dramatic—even better than she had hoped.

"Will you tell us what's going on here?" Monica confronted her, hands on her hips.

"Chill out, big sister. You'll find out soon enough."

"O-o-o-h, I could just kill you, Jessica Anne Nelson," was the furious response.

"Now, now, big sister. Is that a nice thing for a good *Christian* girl to say?"

Before the argument mushroomed, the lights dimmed, a drum roll silenced the audience chatter, and a spotlight pierced the darkened stage, shining on a beautiful, slender woman whose well-known face caused waves of gasps and whispers around the room. Teens crowded around the stage, boys and girls cheered and whistled, chanting in unison, "An-gel! An-gel! An-gel!" The star held her pose until the audience quieted.

She beckoned one of her dancers, who joined her and embraced her tightly to his body. The music broke into a Salsa, and the couple danced vigorously and brilliantly.

When the dance ended, Angel moved downstage. Turning her back, she ripped off her floor length skirt and tossed it offstage, baring her legs from her thighs to her spike heels. Her loosened flaxen hair cascaded over her shoulders and chest. The stage and ballroom darkened. Drums and amplified guitars beat out several measures of her latest hit. She grasped the cordless microphone handed to her and belted out the song. From the waist down, her body moved sinuously to the beat of the music. The lyrics of the seductive love song induced excited grins from the boys and open-mouthed, envious stares from the girls.

Monica slid lower in her chair, her eyes fixed on the floor. Jess grinned at her sister's embarrassment, enjoying every minute of it.

Glancing at Jess, hatred flashed from Monica's eyes and she whispered, "This is the last straw. I'll never allow you to humiliate me again—oh-my-God, they're leaving."

Monica rushed after Pastor Ames and his wife, who had left their table quietly. She caught up with them at the exit, the tip of her ears to her neck pink with embarrassment. Jess could see her apologizing all the way to the lobby.

Kevin followed Monica. Harry remained at the table with Jess, although his head often turned toward the stage.

When Angel's song ended, the excited teens whistled and cheered, refusing to let her leave the stage, so she sang a couple of encores.

"C'mon Harry. Let's get closer so we can invite her to our table when she's through. I'll introduce you. After all, she's *my* guest and *my* birthday present."

After the last song, Angel waited until the cheers and shouts quieted and said, "Thanks so much, guys and gals." Turning, she graciously applauded her backup singers, dancers, and band. She beckoned a male dancer from the group.

"Let me introduce my dance partner, Kostas Carpenter — a new member of our troupe who came all the way from Romania. Isn't he hot, gals?" Screams and applause exploded from the girls in the audience.

They stampeded the stage for autographs. Angel signed a few before a couple of husky dancers hurried her out a rear exit of the ballroom. The pack of fans thundered to the lobby to catch her. Jess and Harry had just reached the stage. In amazement, Jess caught a glimpse of Angel's back as she left. What happened? Disappointment stabbed her heart. Angel's agent hadn't said anything about a limit on the star's time.

Several minutes later, the autograph hounds returned in groups of two or three. The swarming crowd had thinned and the noise had quieted to a conversational buzzing. Many of Monica's youth group had gone home, no doubt thinking the party was over when the pastor and his wife left.

The hired band, Junior and the Jammers, had returned and were setting up their equipment for the final set.

Jess stood at the edge of the stage, unsure of what to do next.

She glanced over to the ballroom entrance. The hotel manager, her dad, Monica, and Kevin walked purposefully toward her. No one looked happy.

"Jessica, are you responsible for the uproar that just happened here?"

"I didn't expect this to happen, Dad—I just thought it would be a nice surprise for everybody." Smiling her brightest and best, she added, "Besides, they're gone and almost everybody is back for the rest of the party."

Eric searched her eyes—the type of look that made her squirm with guilt. At last, he said, "All right. We'll continue the party, but your mother and I will talk to you later. Your mom is on her way."

He turned to leave, but said, "Oh, by the way, you owe the manager here an apology for disturbing the hotel guests."

She apologized and they left.

The two couples returned to their table. Monica's face was tear-streaked, but she was calm. No one spoke or looked at each other. Each stared at the dancers out on the floor.

After a few moments, a bellman approached their table and informed Jess in a low voice she had a phone call. *Now, who would call me on the hotel line?* She opened her evening bag. Yep, her cell was there, it was on, and there were no messages. She frowned. She hoped it wasn't bad news. Unexpected phone calls always meant bad news.

⌘   ⌘   ⌘

Back at the table, Monica's head throbbed with each beat of the drums. She hoped she wasn't getting a migraine. If she didn't, it would be a miracle considering the noise, bright lights, and her anger. She tried to regain her composure so Kevin and Harry wouldn't ask too many questions. She thanked God Jess had left for a little while so she could calm down and not cause a scene. For sure, though, she'd throttle her when they got home. She said a quick prayer for God's forgiveness for her angry thoughts, but her sister had a way of pushing her over the edge.

Many of the guests had left, and deflated balloons drifted around the empty tables like lost souls. A table next to the stage held a precarious stack of unopened gifts. The party was over for her. She'd never live this down.

Kevin's voice—forcing cheerfulness—broke into her thoughts.

"Hey Monica, do you want to dance—or can I get you a fresh Coke?"

Monica shook off her emotions. She should think about somebody else instead of her own pathetic situation.

She smiled and answered, "No thanks, Kevin."

"Jessica's been gone a long time," Harry said, "Should I go look for her?"

Monica straightened, folding her hands on the table. "No, Harry. I'll do it. I'll find her, so we can get on with our plans, and everybody can go home. I'll be back in a minute."

Monica couldn't find Jess in the lobby, rest rooms, restaurants, or any shops inside the hotel. She called up to their room, but no one answered. Her heart thumped. She had a feeling something was terribly wrong.

She approached the desk clerk. "Did you see a girl about sixteen with short, reddish hair and a red evening gown in the last thirty minutes? Except for the hair, she looks like me—we're twins."

He paused, tapping his chin. "Well, yes as a matter of fact I do remember her. A call came in for her at the front desk phone, which I had the operator transfer to one of the house phones, and then sent Rafael to find her." He nodded toward the dark-haired man helping a guest. "A few minutes later, I saw her walk toward the lobby doors like she was waiting for someone."

Monica approached Rafael, the bellman.

"Excuse me, sir. Did you happen to see my sister leave after you brought her to the lobby?"

The bellman replied, "When I unloaded an incoming guest's luggage, I saw her leave in a white limousine. A man in a uniform helped her into the back seat and then drove off."

"A limousine. Did you see who was inside?"

No—excuse me, Miss, I must go. A guest just drove up."

Monica's heart jumped. *We don't know anybody who has a limousine. Is she up to another prank? He said she got in willingly; but what if it just looked like she got in willingly; what if that man had a gun pointed at her so she wouldn't draw attention or scream for help. Maybe they kidnapped her.*

Monica had to find dad or mom right away. She didn't know where they were. Wait …didn't Dad say Mom was on her way? Mom had told her to page her if she needed anything. Well, she needed help right now.

She flipped open her cell. "Mom? This is Monica. Something awful has happened. Jessica's gone. Hurry—and find Dad, too. I'll be waiting by the front desk."

Chapter 10

Up Close and Personal

Jess followed the man out of the ballroom, who directed her toward a secluded area at the lobby's edge.

"You can take your call on a house phone over there," he said.

She waited a moment and then picked up the receiver. "Hello?"

Her caller was Angel. "Hi. I apologize for leaving in such a rush, but I was in the car before I realized I hadn't even talked with you. We are near the hotel and I can have my driver return and pick you up. Can you get away for a little while?"

An irresistible opportunity like that? No way would she miss it.

After Jess had agreed and hung up, she felt guilty. *I should tell Monica and Harry, but there's no time. Oh well, Angel said we wouldn't be gone long.*

It was the first time Jess had ridden in a limousine. Settling into the seat facing Angel, she caressed the supple leather and inhaled its mellow scent. Insulated from the traffic noise, she felt untouched by the world—as if in a cocoon.

"Would you like a Coke or juice? Help yourself, there's plenty." Angel leaned forward and opened the door of a small refrigerator.

Jess shook her head.

Her hostess leaned back. Saying nothing, intelligent green eyes evaluated Jess. At last, she nodded approval and smiled. She had removed her makeup, exposing her complexion, clear and fair. Jess could not believe how great she looked this close. Suddenly, she hated her own dark hair, freckled nose and tanned face.

Angel said, "First, I'd like to get to know you better—by the way, that hair style looks good on you. It's a soft punk style, and your face and eyes are just right for it."

Jess felt a bit better about her looks, considering the compliment from a woman who looked like Angel, but couldn't say anything coherent now. The whole scene seemed like a dream, but better.

"Tell me where you grew up, about your mom and dad, your friends, where you plan to go to college. You know, just about your normal life. My parents were actors, but they both died in an accident when I was young. I don't have sisters or brothers. A distant cousin gave me a home until I signed with A.P. We weren't very close. Once I got on TV, there were plenty of people around, but they aren't family."

"Yes. I read about the accident. I'm sorry. It must be hard to lose both your parents."

"Well, it was a long time ago. I've dealt with it. Do you have any brothers and sisters?"

"I have a twin sister and that's enough for me."

Jess changed the subject. "You're rich and famous and have everything anybody could ever want. You've traveled all over the world. Why would you be interested in a dull, ordinary person like me?"

"Oh, come on—indulge me for awhile; and then, I'll answer *your* questions—maybe even tell you something the Paparazzi hasn't found out."

Jess searched Angel's eyes and found no mockery there. The bottled-up tension of her own troubles spilled out in an angry rush. Her mother was *always* on her case, her dad *never* stuck up for her and her sister *snooped* and *spied* on her.

"So, you can see how my parents don't understand me," she concluded. "They never encourage me—neither does my sister. She just makes fun of me when they're not around. She behaves like the perfect child in front of them. Out of their sight, she's just vicious and mean and—get this—pretends she's lily white because she goes to church. What a hypocrite."

"Do I detect some hostility there? Sounds like you two don't get along at all."

"Right, but I don't want to talk about that. I want to talk about a career someday as a singer or dancer. That's what I want more than anything in the world."

Angel raised her eyebrows. "Are you that unhappy with your life, Jessica? Have you thought of changing things, making specific plans, taking your life into your own hands?"

"Yeah, but I'm trapped until I'm eighteen. I want to sing and dance, Angel—it's all I've wanted since I was a little girl and watched you on that TV show on the Disney channel, *Angela's Army.* I didn't miss an episode—and I still watch the re-runs."

"I'd almost forgotten about that. It was a long time ago."

Angel's attention drifted. She stared out the window submerged in her own thoughts. There was a long pause.

Uncomfortable, Jess fidgeted. She glanced at her watch and realized an hour had passed.

"Excuse me—can we go back now? I've been gone a long time without telling anyone. They're probably looking for me by now."

Angel turned her head and said, "Oh, of course. I was enjoying our visit so much I didn't realize how much time had passed. How selfish of me," she added.

She tapped on the dividing window and ordered the driver to return to the hotel.

"But—before we get back," said Angel, "—may I ask you a couple of very personal questions? You don't have to answer if you don't want to, but in a strange way, I feel a strong bond between us—like we've known each other a long time. I think we're going to become very good friends."

Angel avoided Jess's eyes. Choking back tears—an emotion expressed that took Jess by surprise—she whispered, "You know it's been a long, long time since I've had a good friend to talk to. Did you know today is my birthday, too?"

"Happy birthday." Jess cleared her throat, embarrassed for blurting out all her own problems—and now, Angel's surprising confession. She set aside her feelings of unease. "Sure, go ahead—ask away."

Dabbing her eyes with a tissue, Angel took a deep breath. "Okay, here goes. Question number one: do you have a steady boyfriend?"

Jess shook her head.

"Question number two: Have you ever …" Angel cleared her throat. "…ever had sex with a guy?"

Jess felt the heat in her cheeks and her uneasiness increased, coiling in the pit of her stomach. *What kind of question is that? This is starting to be a little weird.* "Why are you asking me that?"

Angel looked at her own reflection in the window and answered, "Oh, I'm not sure, but I've often wondered what goes on in an average girl's life." She sighed, and then said, "I'm so tired of the mobs and not going anywhere or doing anything without a bodyguard. I've never had a genuine boyfriend, you know, or girlfriends." She stared at Jess, awaiting an answer.

"Well, the answer is no. My parents would kill me. Yeah, many girls my age already have, but not my friends as far as I know. Everybody knows the gang girls do—. I heard that's part of their initiation into the gang. There are other fast crowds that do, but I'm not risking *my* life or future by getting pregnant or getting AIDS."

The limo arrived at the hotel. Angel brought out a small notepad and jeweled pen from her handbag. She scribbled a number on it. "Here. This is my private cell number—it's with me day and night. Call me anytime and we'll work something out for dinner in my suite and talk some more—I'm at the Warwick."

Jess hesitated. She wondered why, of all people, Angel had invited her for such an intimate meeting, or hinted about having a friendship. She didn't want anything more, did she? Yet, the request was irresistible, and curiosity about how the rich and famous lived won out. Besides, if she was a movie star, she had other people around her all the time. Her troubling question didn't mean anything; she'd be safe—as long as nobody knew about it at home.

Jess took the slip of paper and pushed it inside her bra. "Yes. Thank you. You said anytime?"

"Of course. If I'm busy I'll have it turned off, but no one else takes my calls and you may leave a message."

"Okay. Goodbye," said Jess. The driver opened the door and she stepped outside.

⌘　⌘　⌘

Angel waited a few minutes and then retrieved her cell phone from her handbag. She told the man who answered, "Sir, my instructions are to tell you the choice is made." She didn't understand what the message meant, but she didn't dare ignore A.P.'s instructions.

She listened and said, "Oh yes, sir, she is. That's what she said and I believe her. It will probably be several weeks before we can make all the arrangements, but we'll be ready by the date you gave us."

Angel listened another moment before she said, "Yes, I'll let him know. You'll hear from us when we arrive in London." She replaced the cell in her bag, shuddering at the distasteful errand forced upon her.

She hadn't met this contact, but his snobbish tone felt like sandpaper rubbing her skin. She despised herself because she had manipulated Jess on purpose. *God, why did I agree to do this?* In her heart, Angel knew she had no choice. Philomena and A. P. controlled her career, finances, and security. Only eighteen, she felt old, without a future. A. P.'s devious plans for exploiting Jessica left a cold lump in the pit of her stomach. She felt caught in the middle of gathering storm clouds.

Opening the dividing window, she told the driver to take her back to her hotel.

Angel closed and locked the door inside her suite and walked to the mini-bar tucked in an out-of-the-way corner of the living room. She reached for the bottle of amber liquid that would ease her guilt and poured herself a drink. She emptied the glass in two swallows and poured another.

She raised the glass in a toast and said, "Cheers, and happy birthday to me."

Chapter 11

A Misunderstanding

Jess stepped off the Metro train and waited for it to move on before she crossed the street. She checked her watch. Nine o'clock. Probably too early for Angel to be awake, but she'd wait if she must. At intervals for the last two weeks, Jess had tried reaching Angel at the number she gave her after the party. She'd left messages, but they went unanswered.

Now that she was here, Jess's thoughts became anxious. *She did say call her anytime. She did say she kept her personal cell with her all the time.* In desperation, she had decided to see her in person. She could find the Warwick and she'd find Angel. Short of breaking and entering, she'd get into her room somehow. There were many ways she could see her. When Angel recognized her, everything would be all right. There was no way she'd tell her parents and sister about the details of her discussion with Angel. She had planned a temporary escape for early Sunday morning, because, like clockwork, Monica left for Sunday school before eight and her parents slept until at least noon. Officially, her term of restriction wasn't over.

She smiled, thinking about the irony. She recalled that when she and Monica were six, their parents *forced* them to attend Sunday school. At that age, Jess didn't understand why she and Monica must go and her parents could stay home. Her mom had said, "Because I said so. There will be no further discussion about it." She had asked Dad, too, but he answered, "Do what your mother said." They had often teamed up like that.

She looked over at the Warwick Hotel, a Victorian structure known for hosting presidents and royalty. She glanced down at her faded Calvin Kleins and almost lost her nerve. *I should have dressed up so I wouldn't stand out. Oh, well.*

Shrugging off her backpack, she tried dozing, but her thoughts raced. Trying to relax, she replayed in her mind the evening when she had reclined in soft leather seats of a limousine and heard a *movie star* invite her for lunch and a cozy chat in her hotel. After all the misery she'd been through the past two weeks, she *needed* a friend.

I'm sure it's not a practical joke and Angel really likes me. After all, she gave me her private number. Jess rummaged through her pack and found her cell. Removing the card from a pocket in her jeans, she called again.

After ten rings on three tries, she gave up. *Now what?* A patrol car slowed and made a fast U-turn in her direction. Her pulse rate went up.

"Uh-oh. He's coming to check me out." Thinking fast, an idea came to her. She jumped to her feet and waved to the Warwick door attendant as if they were old friends. Shrugging on her backpack, she glanced behind her as she ran to the startled man. Relieved, she saw the patrol car move on.

"Hold on, young lady, are you a guest at the hotel?" The attendant barred her way.

Jess lifted her chin. Bluffing, she said, "I'm a personal friend of Angel, the movie star who lives here, and she invited me to join her for breakfast in her suite. Will you call and let her know Jess Nelson has arrived?"

The attendant eyed her suspiciously. "Yeah. I've heard that one before. Just move on, young la—"

Jess brushed past him and stepped into a wedge of the revolving door. The man followed her and grabbed her arm before she dashed to the elevators.

"Don't touch me," she said, jerking her arm from his grip. "I have her card with her private number on it, and whether you believe me or not, she *did* invite me to her suite."

Jess handed him the card on which Angel had written her number.

The attendant stepped back, looking doubtful. "Well, okay, but wait over there while I check." He nodded toward a fragile, antique chair padded with brocade.

She stalked over to the chair, hoping her bluff worked. She didn't want to start a scene, with cops and all that.

The desk clerk approached her. His polite smile didn't warm his blue eyes. "Young woman, I'm terribly sorry but we have strict orders not to disturb Miss Angel until noon. Perhaps you're mistaken about the time."

"I'm *not* mistaken. I just had a conversation with her less than thirty minutes ago, and she said to come as soon as I could get away." She picked up her backpack and started toward the elevators.

The clerk blocked her way. "No need to do that, Miss. I'll send someone up with a note." He handed her a pad of hotel stationery and gave her a gold pen from the inside of his jacket. She scribbled a note to Angel and folded it several times before she handed it to him.

While she waited, she reflected on the downhill mess of her life since her birthday party. She was through with her hateful sister and unfair parents. It was like living in prison. The events unfolded in her mind's eye.

⌘ ⌘ ⌘

The minute she had stepped out of Angel's limousine, they were waiting for her. Remembering, humiliation crawled through her again.

In front of everybody, her mother had screamed at her.

"You ungrateful brat! How dare you pull a stunt like you did tonight—then have the nerve to take off without saying a word to anybody."

A Misunderstanding

"But Mom—"

"—Not another word. You be ready to check out by eight sharp tomorrow morning." She turned on her heel and stormed to the elevators.

Out of the corner of her eye, she saw some of the kids from the party. It would be all over school next week.

"Daddy ?"

It broke her heart to see the hurt in his eyes. An aching lump settled in her throat.

He had told her, "Jessica, this time I agree with your mother. We're grounding you. You're restricted from leaving the house after school and on weekends for a month. We're disconnecting your computer and taking away your cell phone."

The punishment restrictions didn't hurt her as much as disappointing her father.

⌘ ⌘ ⌘

Earlier that morning in the Warwick penthouse suite, Philomena jerked the bedroom drapes open. Angel opened one eye and squeezed it shut again. Sunlight seared her left temple. She moaned, waving her away.

"Go away, Philomena. It's not time to get up."

Unsympathetic to her moans, she ripped the bedding from under her. "Hmmmph. Hung over. I didn't bring you up to be such a fool. Git your precious butt out of bed."

Hateful witch, thought Angel. With one hand covering her left eye and the other pressing the small of her back, she stumbled into the bathroom.

The hot shower stung, bringing her awake. As her brain fog cleared, she remembered bits and pieces from her concert last night. Maybe she had drunk too much, but nobody noticed. She finished the concert—didn't she? More fog cleared, and a faint echo of a booing audience and someone helping her stumble offstage crept into her mind. Self-pity and shame streamed over her. *Oh, why don't I just go ahead and die?*

She turned off the hot water, and let the cold spray jolt her. Something else had happened that brought so much pain to her conscience that she finished off a bottle of scotch before the concert to anesthetize and forget. Sober this morning, she remembered every guilty detail of her part in the scheme for an innocent young girl. She took advantage of that girl. What was her name? Yes, yes, it was Jessica, the one who had called her and left messages for the last two weeks. She hadn't returned the girl's calls, hoping she'd give up and go away. Now—especially after last night's debacle—she knew someone watched her all the time and knew who that someone was.

"Philomena—the Jamaican Queen, master mind-controller, and guardian of the heavily insured body of Angel, the hot, international star of TV and movies," she muttered.

A Misunderstanding

Steam wafted out the door as Philomena walked in holding a tray with a cup of coffee, a sheaf of papers, and a small, unsealed envelope. "Here's your coffee, and something A.P. wants you to look over."

Angel nodded toward the envelope. "What's that?"

"This was under your door when I came in this morning. I suppose the hotel brought it up, and when they couldn't rouse you they stuck it under your door."

"Who's it from?"

"How would I know–it's to you. You may think I spy on you, but I don't read your mail. I know what goes on in your head anyway. Don't need to bother; I'll just find out later."

Angel sipped her coffee, dropping her eyes to hide her feelings. She set her cup on the tray and took the envelope.

Philomena picked up a thick towel and held it out for Angel. Resentment toward Philomena seethed, and it took every ounce of nerve to look at her and order her to leave. She said in her best measure of firmness, "Okay, Philomena, you may go now. I'm not ready to get out."

Philomena gave the towel an impatient shake. "Oh yes you are, Missy, and stop your uppity ways. You and I have to talk about your drinking problem. Your life destiny is at stake, and you must focus your mind—there's a purpose for you set out by the gods."

"I don't care. You don't own me."

Philomena folded the towel and sat in a nearby chair. "Okay. We'll talk here, but we *will* talk."

Angel surrendered, sliding lower in the tub. Trapped. Too many years under the power of this woman had worn down her spirit.

"You seem to forget who you were when you showed up on my doorstep for the first time—a 13-year-old runaway with the police on her heels. You were nothing. You had nothing but the clothes on your back, penniless, and homeless."

"Yeah, but you made it clear very soon your heart wasn't full of charity," reminded Angel.

"That's true. Now, when it's time to pay homage to the gods for *their* generosity, you want to run away. You *cannot* provoke their anger and invite their wrath." The woman's normal light-brown complexion darkened, a warning preceding a hard slap across her face.

Despite the warm water, Angel shivered. She hated it when she talked about the "gods, casting spells," or her voodoo priestess language. Her skin crawled every time. When she was younger and had crossed her, unexplainable things happened—a broken ankle, a failing grade, and nightmares.

If you cooperate with our plan perhaps they will look kindly upon you again."

Philomena caught Angel's eyes with a hypnotic gaze, speaking in a low monotone, "Alcohol weakens the will. The herbs bring strength—superhuman strength, and I will teach you about them. We will begin tomorrow."

A Misunderstanding

Philomena released her hypnotic spell, rose and replaced the chair. "I have to go out for a few hours. I suggest you spend your time constructively while I'm gone." She nodded toward the music sheets and left.

Angel sighed and reached for the music. She saw the envelope, which stimulated her curiosity. Who sent her a note on hotel stationery? She unfolded the note and read:

Angel. I desperately need to talk to you. You said if I needed to talk, contact you. I'm downstairs now. Will you see me? Jessica Nelson.

Angel groaned. "Oh no. She didn't give up after all. That means the plan must continue." She reached for the towel, drying herself on her way to the dressing table with the house phone.

⌘　⌘　⌘

In the lobby, Jessica snapped out of her daydreaming when she heard a polite cough from the bellman. He held out an envelope.

"Miss Angel sent this note for you."

Jess tipped him and unfolded the note.

Give me about ten minutes to arrange for us to be alone. Take the elevator to the penthouse suite and I'll let you in. Λ.

Ten minutes felt like hours and Jess checked her watch every few minutes. At last, she stood at the suite door and rang the bell. When Angel opened the door, Jess caught her breath in wonder. *At last, I'm here. I can't wait to see what it looks like.* She stepped into a tiled and mirrored foyer, then three steps leading to a sunken, spacious living room covered with tightly woven white carpet. She left her sneakers and backpack on the marbled foyer floor. Floor to ceiling windows with opened drapes framed a great view of the southern edge of the city. Wow. The luxury enveloped her with loving arms. She made a promise to herself. *This is exactly what I'll have someday.*

"You like my little playhouse?"

Angel, wrapped in a thick terry cloth robe, rubbed her hair with a towel.

"Forgive me. My maid brought me your note as I was bathing. I sent her out on an errand that will take at least an hour. We'll have time to talk alone."

She tucked the towel turban-style around her head and reached for Jess's hands, urging her to sit on the sofa and help herself to anything on the silver tray.

Jess sat, feeling a little dizzy. Angel searched her eyes. "You look a little pale. Here, sit down and eat some eggs and toast. I bet you haven't eaten much." She continued toweling her hair and turned toward her bedroom. "Finish breakfast while I get dressed. When I get back I want you to tell me everything that's going on with you."

A Misunderstanding

Jess poked the eggs with her fork. She wasn't hungry. After she tasted the first bite of the fluffy omelet, hunger kicked in and she cleaned the plate, realizing she hadn't eaten anything since yesterday morning.

When Angel returned, she had changed to running shoes, shorts, and tank top.

"Okay friend, tell me what's going on. I'll listen while you talk." Angel curled up in the opposite corner of the sofa, nibbling on a stalk of celery from a glass of tomato juice.

"Oh, I'm sorry. I'm keeping you from your run—"

"—Sit down. I can take my run later. I meant what I told you. I want us to be friends, and friends help each other out, don't they?"

Jess settled back into the sofa, feeling safe and comfortable. She took a deep breath and began.

"When I left you after that night of my party, my parents and hotel security guard waited in the lobby. I thought my parents would understand after I explained about your call, but they wouldn't listen and grounded me for a month. It wasn't fair."

She looked at her clenched hands and then brushed angry tears from her eyes. "There's more."

"Okay, go on."

Gulping back more tears she said, "Two weeks ago I got in trouble at school for fighting and I was grounded for that." This time they took away my cell phone, computer, after school activities. I can't leave my room except for school and meals. They've got me in *solitary*," she wailed.

Angel patted her hand like a big sister. "But here you are. Obviously, you can escape. It can't be all that bad."

"But it wasn't my fault—I didn't start the fight; she asked for it– spreading all those awful lies about me."

"Lies?"

"Yes, lies. Rumors about me all over the school."

"Like what?"

"That I was pregnant by some guy I'd been sneaking out with."

Angel's eyes widened. "Is it true?"

"No, it's a lie, and I know *exactly* who started it"

"Who? Your sister?"

"No. Just my best friend, Pam, knew about that night with Eddie. It *had* to be her."

"Eddie? I thought you said you didn't have a boyfriend."

Jess's face reddened. "I don't. He was just a date. I mean, I don't mean–. We didn't have sex. In fact, he tried to rape me. I got away and I've never seen him again. Pam and her boyfriend double-dated with Eddie and me that night and she borrowed her boyfriend's car and drove me home. I didn't want anyone to call the police because I wasn't hurt—just a little shook up. Neither of the guys go to our school and I didn't tell anybody else about it. So, you see, it had to be Pam."

Angel stood abruptly and walked away—something had upset her. Her quick mood swing took Jess off guard. *Now I've blown it. I shouldn't have told her about Eddie. I've probably disgusted her.* She stared at the floor when tears welled up.

Peeping through her lashes, she watched Angel walk to the windows, silent and distant.

Unable to tolerate Angel's unexplainable coldness, Jess quietly put on her sneakers, grabbed her backpack, and slipped out unnoticed.

Alone in the elevator, Jess let go of her tears. Angel was her last hope. Lowering her head, she rushed out of the hotel as if demons chased her.

Chapter 12

Kos, the Mystery Man

Angel turned away from the window. Jess was gone. How much time had passed? Panic gripped her. This strange time lapse…was she losing her mind? She looked at the glass in her hand. *I don't remember fixing a drink.* Shaken, she hurried to the bar and dumped the remains of the Bloody Mary in the sink.

The click of a key, followed by rattling shopping bags startled her. The reflection above the bar mirror verified the visitor was Philomena, who juggled the bags in both arms and kicked the door shut.

"Gal, give me a hand here."

Angel turned on the water and washed her hands, pretending she didn't hear her. Taking some time to compose herself, she didn't turn around right away.

Grumbling, Philomena came behind her and set the bags on the counter. She noticed the melting ice cubes and eyed Angel with suspicion.

She flattened her lips in disapproval. "So now you're drinking before noon."

Angel turned away, ignoring the comment. She glanced around the room. "Now, where's that music that A.P. wants me to look at?"

"You can't fool me; you've been drinking—and don't change the subject."

"No I haven't been drinking. I just had a glass of tomato juice with my breakfast—"

"You need a good dose of my herbs to clear out all that poisonous alcohol in your system."

Angel's back stiffened and something in her snapped. She was so tired of Philomena's bullying.

"Don't you *dare* give me any more of that stuff," she said. She clenched her teeth so hard, pain shot through her jaw.

Angel rushed toward her bedroom and turned, gathering courage to confront Philomena, but chills raised the hair on the back of her neck when her eyes met the wicked gleam in the Jamaican woman's eyes.

Lapsing into her native dialect, she muttered, "You be ver' sorry you crossed me, gel."

Frightened, Angel turned, slammed, and locked her bedroom door.

⌘　⌘　⌘

During the long bus ride home, Jess's unwelcome, depressing thoughts kept her company. Although tired and disappointed, she didn't stay down long. Her natural optimism displaced the negative thoughts. She would *never* give up her dream of becoming a singing star. Jess just knew she could make it without waiting. Mom and dad wanted her to wait until she graduated from college. No way. Everybody knows major MTV stars start in their teens. *Somehow, some way I'll get what I want.*

At home, no one was around and she sneaked into her room without a problem.

A moment before she stepped into the shower, her cell blasted out the rock song announcing an incoming call. She hurried to her dresser, answering before it woke her parents.

"Hello?" She listened a moment, a smile spreading across her face.

"Sure," she answered. "No problem. I shouldn't have left so soon, but I was embarrassed—you know what I mean, don't you?"

Her grin widened. "Wow. I'd love to come back for a late lunch. What time?"

Closing her cell, she thrust her fist upward in the victory sign and said, "YES." She was still solid with Angel. She planted an affectionate kiss on her cell—her spare for grounding emergencies. She stepped into the steamy shower, humming.

⌘ ⌘ ⌘

Locked in her room, Angel slept, worry and fatigue plaguing her following one more disturbing encounter with Philomena's evil side. When she awakened, she felt refreshed and ventured into the sitting room. She had to get hold of herself. She'd be free the rest of the afternoon and evening—at least free to do what she wanted in her own suite. When Philomena returned to the hotel, however, she'd be in the adjoining suite as A.P. had arranged. She couldn't leave the building without a bodyguard. She was certain now she'd be toast if she didn't follow through with her part of the plan, so she found Jess's number on her cell caller I.D., apologized, and invited her back for a late lunch.

In the late afternoon, she received a call from her favorite male—Kos, her dance partner. There was a knock on the door as soon as she answered the call.

She told him, "Hold on a minute, room service is here with lunch."

After the waiter left she continued, "Kos, you can't come here now. I'm expecting a guest any moment. Why, all of a sudden, do you need to go over some routines before our next rehearsal?"

Her face softened as she listened, remembering things about him that she shouldn't if she wanted to keep control of her feelings.

"You're going out of town tomorrow? How long?"

"Two weeks? We've got the London gig in two weeks—"

She paced as she listened.

Frowning, she stopped. "What do you mean you made 'previous plans' you can't cancel? You work for me and my plans are your plans." She looked at her watch. "You be *here* at six—no earlier or no later. Remember, no matter how good you are you can be replaced." Shaking with anger, she threw the cell on the sofa.

She hated playing boss, but she was in charge of hiring and firing her backup dancers and singers. A.P. granted that one responsibility. A.P. controlled her money and Philomena controlled her mind—at least she tried with her voodoo threats, strong will, and strength.

She sighed, rubbing her temples. Sometimes she felt just as trapped and violated as she did with Pa. She wanted to run away from everything, but the question was how. What would she do? Who would help her?

The hotel phone rang. "Yes, send Miss Nelson right up," she replied.

She hung up, drumming her fingernails on the table. "Wait a minute." The drumming stopped. "Hmmm. It just might work."

Smiling, she said to herself, "Okay. Here's what I'm going to do. I'll let Kos in on the plan to a point and offer him a featured spot in my show—an offer no dancer can refuse—if he gains her trust and persuades her to come easily to the company within the next two weeks."

Kos didn't have to know everything, and he's a man. Even if the girl was young, she appeared older and she was good-looking. As for herself, she couldn't go on lying to her. She had told so many lies about her own past and an interest in befriending her that she hadn't the stomach for one more lie to the unsuspecting girl. However, Angel knew she couldn't get out of what A.P. and Philomena told her to do. They watched every move she made and she wanted out.

I can stand their spying for two weeks until we get to London. Then I'll think of something. She didn't want to know any more details about the trap her agent and guardian had set for Jessica either.

The doorbell rang. She walked to the cart and lifted the domed cover of the platter. Pizza with the works. She thought it was a great menu choice for lunch with a sixteen-year-old. Anyway, she loved pizza. The smell of onions and gooey melted cheese started her saliva flowing. She didn't realize how hungry she was.

Jess and Angel sat on the balcony outside Angel's bedroom, a light breeze pushing the curtains in a graceful dance.

"A toast," said Angel, "to the beginning of a beautiful friendship."

Time sped by while they chatted. Later, Angel suggested Jess think about joining their company. Angel turned and studied her, commenting, "You have a great look—athletic and strong—and a lot of ambition. You'll fit in."

Jess's face brightened. "When?"

"Well, it's up to you to get your parents to sign some papers. It shouldn't be hard because you will continue your education on the road. Can you do it in two weeks? We'll start you right away with dancing and singing lessons. I think I can manage to work it out with my manager to sign you before we go back on the road in a couple weeks."

"Awesome," responded Jess, grinning.

Angel stood at the balcony rail and turned her back on Jess. Her conscience handed her a big dose of guilt. Any hope of fixing the damage already done was gone. She needed a drink.

The hotel phone rang. Angel felt relieved by the distraction. Looking at her watch and excusing herself, she went inside.

"Send him up," she told the caller. Apparently, Kos had decided to come early. Oh well.

She stuck her head through the curtains, suggesting, "Why don't we come back inside? It's getting chilly, and I have someone coming up I want you to meet."

A few minutes later, Jess rubbed pizza crumbs off her jeans, holding out her hand to Kos when Angel introduced them.

Angel observed both during her introductions, aware of the excited light in Jess's eyes and smile. She suppressed the flash of jealousy that came up, reasoning, *this is good. One look and she's hooked.* And, why not? With his dark hair, sexy eyes, and graceful carriage, he was any woman *or* girl's dream.

Did she see a little too much interest show in *his* eyes during introductions?

She dismissed her edginess and returned her attention to her plans. She'd find out soon enough.

The three sat on the large sofa facing the windows. Angel and Kos settled at the curved ends and Jessica in the middle. Settling back, Angel had a clear view of both and watched the interaction between them. Choosing the right moment for her exit was important. She had already decided she would take advantage of Jess's vulnerability to the charms of Kos Carpenter.

After a few moments of idle talk, Angel sensed warming in the atmosphere between Jess and Kos. She stood and glanced at her watch. "Oh, my gosh, look at the time. I almost forgot. A.P. set me up for an interview at the recording studio. I'm so sorry about this."

On her way out, she said, "Kos, why don't you call down for dessert—whatever Jessica wants—and you, too. I'll be back in an hour, or sooner if I can."

Jess stared at her, a shocked expression on her face.

Angel noticed, and added, "Don't worry. It's not unusual to leave my friends alone here. They're my friends and I trust them."

⌘　⌘　⌘

Jessica's heart raced with anticipation. The moment he had greeted her with his natural European charm, she melted.

With the same courtesy, he stood when Angel left. He returned to his seat on the sofa and asked, "What would you enjoy for dessert, Jessica?"

He looked into her eyes with such intensity she felt like the most important person in the world. Her thoughts were giddy. *I think he's attracted to me. This is a dream—he is a dream.* She came to her senses and realized he had asked her a question.

"Oh. Uh—anything is okay with me."

Deep in her belly, Jessica felt something alien and new. Thinking he might read her embarrassing thoughts, she rose and walked to the large window, pretending fascination with the sunset.

Without waiting, he called and ordered dessert. He glanced at her. "Would you mind if I ordered for you?"

She nodded her tongue unable to speak a coherent sentence.

Fifteen minutes later, Kos admitted a waiter who presented a dessert named *Cherries Jubilee*. She hadn't tasted the dessert before because it had alcohol in it. She took a bite, which slid down her throat and left a pocket of warmth in the pit of her stomach. Her head felt light, but she didn't know if it was the brandy or the crazy feelings she had when near him.

Kos picked up a spoon and took a bite, too. Five minutes later, the platter was clean. Jess remembered nothing after the first bite.

"Um-m-m. That was delicious wasn't it," asked Kos.

He put down his spoon and shifted to a more comfortable position. He stared at her for a long time, then asked, "How old are you, Jessica."

"Eighteen." She surprised herself at how the lies slithered past her tongue.

"Are you a dancer? You have the look of one and you're very attractive." He reached into his shirt pocket, pulled out a card, and held it out to her.

"Here. Take my card. I have my cell number written on the back. If you need an instructor, I can direct you to some good ones and get you connected in no time."

Jess felt so buoyed up, she couldn't curb her enthusiasm. "Wow– You are *too* great to do that. Yes, I want to be a dancer. Oh, thank you, thank you, thank you." She leaned over and threw her arms around his neck—

⌘   ⌘   ⌘

"Hi. I'm back earlier than I expected. Give me a minute while I put my things in my room and I'll join you for coffee." Kos removed Jess's arms encircling his neck and rose to his feet.

Angel's gut twisted when she saw Jess pull her arms away from Kos's neck and move away. There no doubt Jess was infatuated. It was what she planned wasn't it? Yet, she wondered about Kos's feelings. Did he initiate the embrace she interrupted?

She decided to let it go and keep her feelings out of it. She would keep matters on business when they were alone.

Chapter 13

A Tarnished Star

Jess had rushed out, mumbling apologies that she couldn't stay for coffee. As soon as the door closed, Angel walked to the windows, her back to Kos. She *must* regain control of her emotions. Until then she couldn't look at him.

"Would you mind if I changed in there in your dressing room," he asked.

"Change?" She turned and stared at him, mystified.

"Yes. That's why I'm here, isn't it—to go through some routines before I leave town?"

"Oh, of course. Yes, yes. I forgot."

After he closed the bedroom door, she returned to the windows. The late afternoon sun blazed between the skyscrapers and she drew the drapes. Her thoughts drifted to the man in her bedroom, wondering why he, and no other man, made her legs weak when she looked into his eyes. Up to now, she hadn't become emotionally entangled with men—attractive men. He disturbed her, but she'd never admit it.

She would get out of all the mess she'd gotten herself into—she had to. *No man—any man—will control me again. Pa whipped the love out of me. A.P. may control my money, but never kill my spirit.*

Stealthy as a panther, Kos was behind her and said, "Okay, I'm ready. Where will we do this?"

Angel started, feeling as if he could read her mind. She hurried to the bar and took a couple of glasses from the shelf. Her hands trembled. Without turning she asked, "Would you like a drink before we start."

"I'll pass."

"Well, I'll have one if you don't mind." She took a swallow and her confidence returned.

Gesturing to the sofa she said, "Why don't we talk a few minutes? I have a business proposition to make to you."

She sat on the sofa, drawing one leg beneath her. Kos straddled a straight-backed chair, positioning it so the coffee table separated them.

She concocted her story as she went along. "Uh—A.P. had this idea that if I befriended one of my fans and took her on our next tour as a trainee and publicize it, fan interest and attendance would increase. He says ticket sales are down for some reason."

"Okay. So that's your agent's idea; what's *your* proposal?"

"I'm getting to that. Time is short and I have recording commitments and interviews, leaving little time to work with her. Unfortunately, it's too late to select someone else, because we go on the road in two weeks."

Something in his eyes told her he didn't believe her.

She rose and rinsed her glass at the bar.

She proceeded, "If you agree, I'll offer you co-star billing—naturally, with a substantial salary increase. In return, spend your spare time coaching her in basic routines and—uh—softening her up so she'll join us now instead of waiting several years. She does show some talent."

Kos gazed at his hands. "Hmmm, that's funny. I told her the same thing. She does look like a quick study. What's keeping her from going now?"

Angel continued, avoiding his question. "She is ambitious and quite a schemer and needs a little push to go after what she wants. Right now, she seems—uh—a bit reluctant. I think you will be better suited to this than I will. It will help both of you in your careers."

Kos narrowed his eyes and said, "Let me guess—she's under age and you want me to mislead her that I'm interested in her romantically?"

Angel nodded.

Kos stroked his chin.

"Oh, I see now. This is a scheme to manipulate *me* into something *you* don't want to do." He stood abruptly, setting the chair aside. Angel physically felt the impact of the psychological wall he raised.

"Count me out. Your story has as many holes in it as Swiss cheese. Why lie to her? Why encourage her to disobey her parents? She's still a schoolgirl—jail bait, for God's sake."

Shaking his head, he walked to the bedroom to change. "Get someone else. I don't want to get involved."

Angel panicked. She'd told so many lies and half-truths she'd forgotten what was true and what was not.

"Wait—" She caught his arm.

He paused but didn't turn around.

"If I tell you something else very important, will you at least think about it some more?" Self-disgust squirmed within her.

"I'm listening." He turned around, his expression unreadable.

She told him everything—at least what she wanted him to know. "A.P. controls my money and career because of a trust fund I can't touch until I'm twenty one. Philomena spies on me, too, watching every move I make.

Kos said, "Philomena? Who is she?"

"Well, it's a long story, but she is the last person I can count as my family—a servant in our household since I was born. My parents were killed when I was thirteen, and she took care of me so I wouldn't be put in foster homes." More lies. She lowered her eyes and took a moment. It gave her time to think.

"—But that's not all," she went on, "I don't understand how Philomena did it, but she has custody of me until I'm twenty-one and controls the property I inherited from my parents."

"So, what does all this have to do with persuading a sixteen-year-old schoolgirl to leave her family and home town? She told me she was eighteen and had graduated from high school, but I don't believe her."

"Yes, she did lie about her age, as many teenage girls do when they meet an attractive, older man." Angel felt some triumph when his neck reddened. She'd upset him, and that was good.

I can't tell him too much, but he's not taking the bait. I won't mention my suspicions about their underlying plans, or my own plans to escape. Finally, Angel decided she'd tell him the truth—at least some of it.

Looking steadily into his eyes, she said, "All right. I didn't want to say anything at first because I have nothing solid to prove my suspicions."

Kos relaxed; he guided her to the sofa and sat next to her.

"Okay. Talk to me some more. Just what are your suspicions and who are you suspicious of?"

Taking a deep breath, Angel replied, "I know the girl is in danger, but I don't know everything. Neither A.P. nor Philomena told me what the whole plan is, but they said they would kill me if I didn't cooperate or if I asked too many questions. I need help to get Jessica and me away from them. I can't report it to the police because those two watch me every moment. But you can."

While she waited for his answer, her stomach knotted like a coiled snake ready to strike.

She raised her eyes to his. Did she see a hint of gentleness there?

He hesitated through a few more heartbeats before he said, "Okay, but if I find out something is wrong, I'll be gone."

She released her breath. He said nothing more and continued on his way out. There was nothing more to say. After he left, Angel opened the drapes and stared at the pinpricks of light in the deepening dusk, wondering what would happen now.

⌘　⌘　⌘

Kos stepped into the elevator. As the elevator descended, he carefully processed the new information. The car was empty, eliminating distractions. Kos's real identity was Kostas Karpati, Special Agent, FBI. Currently, he was on undercover assignment in connection with The International Task Force, a joint effort by the United States and European countries investigating child sex trafficking activities throughout Eastern Europe. At twenty-five, he was the youngest member on the team. Today, while he changed clothes, he had succeeded planting cameras and microphones in Angel's suite. He went undercover for evidence that Angel and her manager were the American link with a ring of international sex traffickers. He needed more time, because he hadn't gained access to the agent's quarters and business office to plant microphones and cameras. According to his background check on Angel, he knew she lied about her family. She ran away from a small town and took up residence with the woman called Philomena. Now the latest turn of events muddied what he had thought a clean assignment. He hadn't anticipated an unsuspecting teenaged victim already selected for abduction and delivery. He knew he had to get her out of the trap set for her, so he improvised the plan of teaching her some dance routines. Nevertheless, he had to get the information to headquarters right away. Angel's confession about death threats forcing her cooperation with the conspiracy changed the picture, too, but she may be lying about that as well. He needed time, just a little more time, and he must not blow his cover. If the operation extended outside the States, which looked like it would, he'd be outside the protection of the U.S. Government.

The elevator doors opened to the lobby.

⌘　⌘　⌘

After Kos closed the door, silence crowded the room. An evening and a sleepless night stretched before her. Angel's exhausted mind spun. She must shut out haunting memories and mounting fear, or– Maybe she would listen to music or rehearse through some of her songs, watch a film, call someone. Nothing interested her. She didn't want a meaningless chat with someone. She had hangers-on, not friends. She wanted a drink. Nothing else shut out the pain and fear or helped her sleep. She poured another drink, loathing herself.

She took the drink, tucked the half-full bottle under her arm, grabbed the ice bucket, went to her bedroom, and locked the door. She knew it was pointless locking the door because Philomena had a key, but it made her feel better.

She sat Indian style in the middle of the bed, anticipating the delicious numbness from the scotch.

Her thoughts drifted back five years, which, compared to her life now, seemed a time of innocence.

She was thirteen again, a runaway, terrified but determined never to set foot in her hometown again. She didn't miss it. Miss what? A lonely girl named Angela Ross, beaten up by her father every day. Angela Ross had died a long time ago. A nobody buried in No Name, Texas. That nobody, that naïve country girl, uneducated and poor, became *Angel,* star of stage, screen, and TV. She reached her dream, didn't she? She had a bright future, didn't she?

Unchecked, tears streamed down her cheeks. She mourned for the freshness of new dreams, hope. Suddenly, sadness became anger. She rubbed the tears from her cheeks with the back of her hand and chugged another drink, not bothering to put ice in her glass. The burning tore her throat, robbing her of breath. She needed some air. When she stepped outside, she stopped coughing and the sensation of burning lava in her throat pooled to a warm glow in her belly. The pleasant feeling dissolved into a strange compulsion. What if she climbed the railing, opened her arms, and leaned forward. Could she fly? Would she be free?

She looked at the sky beyond the washed-out halo around the city lights. Her special star waited in the midnight sky. There were billions out there.

A bruised reed he will not break, and a smoldering wick he will not snuff out. It was as if someone whispered the words in her ear.

Where had she heard that before? Oh yes, it was from the Bible. She remembered the worn, leather-bound Bible Darla carried in her backpack and read to her on lazy Sunday afternoons.

I must stop thinking about all this. It hurts too much. She went inside, drew the drapes, and collapsed on her bed.

Soon, the warm glow radiated to her muscles and brain, bringing dizziness and a heavy feeling in her eyelids. The empty glass slipped from her hand, rolling from her bed to the carpeted floor. The sound of voices roused her from her slide into unconsciousness. She tried opening her eyes and moving her arms and legs, but she could not. Panicking, she thought, *I'm paralyzed.*

She struggled within her mind, but her body didn't cooperate. The lock clicked, and she recognized the voices of A.P. and Philomena next to her bed.

"She's drunk herself into unconsciousness again," said A.P.

She heard him move to another part of her room as if searching for something.

"We'll have to change our plans; I don't have the time or the inclination to determine whether she'll be sober enough to successfully execute her part of our plans. The earl is getting impatient." With an uncharacteristic chuckle he said, "He gets a bonus this time."

"Miss Angel, too? How we goin' do that?" countered Philomena.

"That's up to you. You're the one who knows all the voodoo mumbo jumbo and spell casting. Use it."

"Someday you'll regret your mockery of the dark powers," she hissed.

"Your foolish curses fail to frighten me."

Their voices faded as they moved out of the room.

The paralysis moved through her limbs, her chest, and her brain. *O-o-o-h, no– she slipped a drug into my bottle this morning.* There was a sound like swarming bees in her head; and then, nothing.

Chapter 13

Little White Lies

The next morning, pounding on her door and the muffled voice of her sister awakened Jessica.

"Hey, wake up. Mom and dad want to see us in the kitchen right now."

"All right, all right, I'm awake, I'm coming," she replied.

Jess yawned and snuggled under the covers. "Mmm," she murmured. "Just a few minutes more." Then she bolted upright, registering the importance of the message Monica delivered. A command appearance from both parents meant she was in deep trouble. *Oh-oh. Did they find out I left the house yesterday?* She thought she had been very careful when she left, but she never knew when Monica was snooping. Frowning, she grabbed her robe and slippers.

To Jess's relief, the summons was not a family meeting to dish out more punishment to her. Her mother had invited some important clients for a party. Mom warned both girls that they must stay around but out of the way and they must wear *appropriate* outfits. Both parents kept their eyes fixed on Jessica during the warning. She knew it was their tired old way of showing off their perfect family for important guests. It had started years ago when they were five years old. Mom always dressed them in matching, ruffled outfits. Jess felt like merchandise for an auction.

After introductions and nibbling appetizers, Jess slipped outside by the pool. She sat at the edge, her parentally approved skirt hiked above her knees, feet dangling in the water. Monica sat on the deck near the Tiki lights, reading. The chilly, damp breeze of November raised goose bumps on Jess' bare arms. Earlier, her sleeveless blouse had felt comfortable. She dried her feet with her skirt and slipped on her sandals.

When she passed, Monica made a spiteful remark. "I know you weren't in your room yesterday. Where were you?"

"If I *had* been gone, I wouldn't tell you anyth—"

"—I know how to pick a lock, too."

"Why, you dirty little sneak. What are you doing, spying on me?"

With exaggerated care, Monica set down her book and walked toward Jess, a smug smile on her face.

"Oh, I'm up on just about everything you do these days. You interested?"

Then, in a vindictive manner, Monica stuck her face close to Jess's, whispering, "I know all about your night with Eddie; your little secret phone calls to Pam. Who do you think started the rumors at school?"

Jess's heart pounded, and hatred boiled within her. "You-you mean Pam wasn't the one who told? You broke up our friendship. O-o-o, you two-faced witch."

Monica sidestepped Jess's lunge at her hair.

Nodding toward the patio doors, she warned, "Easy, little sister—you're in enough trouble already."

Her mother looked at them through the patio doors and frowned.

Taking two deep breaths, Jess moved into the shadows, out of sight of the doors, dragging Monica with her.

"Okay–I know you want something, you stupid little blackmailer. What is it?"

"You got kicked off the cheerleading squad, right? They're having tryouts in two weeks for two replacements and I want one of those spots—bad." In her haughtiest tone, Monica said, "Although it *pains* me to admit this, I need your help to polish my routine."

"Why should I help you get my spot on the squad—you're a nothing, talent-less nerd and you wouldn't even make the first cut. Besides, I can get back on the team anytime I want."

Monica turned her back, gazing into the pool, oblivious to her sister's insults. In an even tone, she said, "Your personal opinion about my character doesn't matter to me. Your experience does. Oh, yes one more thing. I think Mom and Dad would be *very* interested you've been sneaking out to see that movie star and you're planning to meet some older guy very soon."

She turned around, her lips curved in a satisfied grin at the shock on Jess's face.

A red haze blinded Jess for a few seconds. She took a step forward—and shoved.

The splash and Monica's screeching stopped the party buzz inside. Within seconds, onlookers gathered around the pool as Eric hauled out a sputtering, drenched teen-ager.

The moment she pushed, Jess had turned and slipped through the back gate. No one saw her or stopped her.

The dewy grass soaked her sandals as she made her way through the neighborhood back yards. The barking dogs didn't bring anyone outside, and she ducked into shadows or bushes whenever a security light flooded a yard.

Having no idea of where she could go, Jess kept walking. After her anger cooled she muttered, "I've blown it. After that two-tongued sneak blabs, I'm ruined. What am I going to do?"

Should she just throw herself on the mercy of her mom and dad? Angel or Kos? How will she get past her lies to Kos? It was just too humiliating. Ideas whirled in and out of her spinning mind.

She had to face her parents sometime. It was late and walking alone on the dark streets frightened her. Murders, rapes, and robberies occurred in quiet Sugar Land neighborhoods, too. She hurried back, furtively looking behind her, avoiding hedges and dark sidewalks, walking in the middle of the unlighted streets.

Spotting the rooftops of her neighbor's house and theirs, Jess expected her house to be ablaze with lights, angry parents and a snotty sister waiting for her—maybe even a couple of squad cars. Instead, the house was in darkness except dim lights left on all night. She entered through the back gate, hidden by wisteria vines and bushes. Uh-oh. She didn't have her key. The "escape window" in her room wasn't open either. After a quick search, she found a window opened several inches in the downstairs study. She removed the screen and wriggled inside.

She stepped on the last step of the stairs, which creaked. She froze, listening. She didn't hear anything and tiptoed through the carpeted hallway to her room.

Passing Monica's room, she spied a slice of light under the door. The slice enlarged to a rectangle when her sister jerked the door open. Monica stood there, arms crossed, wearing her ridiculous Mickey Mouse night shirt, and whispered, "I let you get away with your vicious trick this time—I told them it was an accident *just* because I didn't feel like going into a long explanation about our fight—but you'll pay for that somehow and sometime when you least expect it."

Cutting off anything Jess might say, Monica slammed the door, slid the deadbolt lock in place, and switched off her lights. *Too bad. I had a great comeback to make her even madder.* She went on to her room.

⌘　⌘　⌘

A week later, between second and third periods, Jess ducked into the rest room. She locked a stall, took a wrinkled business card from her bra, and called the number penciled on it.

"Hello?" He answered on the fourth ring.

Her heart pounded and her tongue felt glued to the roof of her mouth. *Oh God, don't blow it, Jess. He's just a guy.* She was sure by the look in his eyes and his passing his cell number and whisper to call was a sign that he liked her—more than liked her, didn't he? She couldn't remember being this uncertain about anything. She couldn't go through with it—

"Hello, hello? Who is this?"

Before another thought stopped her, a flood of words poured forth. "Hi—remember me, Jessica Nelson? We met at Angel's, you said it was okay to call—but if you're busy, I won't bother you. Maybe you've forgotten."

"Whoa—slow down, Jess. Sure, I remember you—I have a vivid memory about it."

She heard the smile in his voice and visualized his dimple. Just the memory of the feel of his broad shoulders when she put her arms around him brought that odd fluttery feeling in her stomach again.

"Oh." She took a deep breath. "I would have called you sooner, but my schedule was packed." She hoped she *sounded* busy *and* older.

"Sure. Don't worry about it."

The pause seemed much too long. She swallowed and tried remembering why she called.

He spoke first. "Look, could you carve out some time from your *busy* schedule and meet me for lunch in about an hour? I want to talk to you."

"An hour? I guess so."

"You know a place called *Angelina's* off Highway 6 and the Interstate?"

"Uh—I'm not sure." Jess thought fast. She'd have to ditch some classes, but this was just too good to miss, so she'd risk it.

"I'll give you the address of the restaurant and the phone number; or, you can call me on my cell. Okay?"

Somehow, she held back her excitement and wrote down the address and phone number on the bit of space left on the card. Hard to believe, but she had a date with him. That incredible thought swept all others from her mind.

After they ended the call, she composed herself. She must make a plan. How can she sneak out the Suburban? Thank heaven her sister wasn't in any of her classes. Since the swimming pool incident, Monica watched her like a cat with its eye on a sparrow. She remembered the extra key in its magnetized case beneath the front fender. Sweet. She would return the SUV before school ended, and Monica wouldn't miss it. *Wait—I forgot about the parking place.* It occurred to her somebody else might park there before she returned.

She rushed to the parking lot. She spotted their Suburban three rows from the last. Her creepy sister remembered *exactly* where they parked every day. She needed an idea.

Then an idea clicked. On the east side of the lot near an open field, bright orange cones caught her eye. Perfect. Now—if, unnoticed, she could just borrow a couple of them. She didn't see any workers around the repaving area. She drew nearer. Several hundred yards away she saw the work crew eating their lunches beneath the shade of a grove of trees.

Ten minutes later, she backed out of the space, jumped out with the cones, and placed two in the vacant space.

As she drove into the restaurant parking lot, Jess congratulated herself for having truancy down to a fine art. She had left school grounds without problems. After Monica had badgered and threatened her to the point of insanity, she gave in and had scheduled her for a coaching session an hour before tryouts, which meant she must be back by four.

Jess removed her compact from her handbag and checked herself out. No lipstick on teeth, hair re-colored to an acceptable auburn shade. She snapped the compact shut and smoothed her skirt.

Kos waited for her. "I hope you like Italian. *Angelina's* is my favorite place. Their veal parmesan is outstanding."

He spoke a few words to the host, who led them to a secluded corner next to a fountain surrounded by large plants. She interpreted his choice as an invitation to romantic intimacy.

Inspired, she imagined herself tall, beautiful, and sophisticated instead of short, "perky" (as her father in his maddening way had labeled her), and sixteen. She lifted her chin and *floated* to the chair Kos held out for her.

However, her self-confidence wilted under his quizzical stare. She felt like squirming.

She cleared her throat. "Well. So, you're from—Romania is it? Tell me about it. It sounds quite mysterious."

A smile twitched the corner of his mouth, further unnerving her. She couldn't think of anything else except to keep talking. His silence was like approaching the black hole in space—unknown.

Jess went on, "What about your family? Do you have brothers and sisters? Are your mom and dad still alive—?"

"—that's a lot of questions before we've even had an appetizer."

The waiter appeared at his elbow with a tray of artfully arranged appetizers. Kos nodded and the waiter offered the tray to Jess, from which she picked a steaming something and nibbled on it. This took care of the conversation void for a moment.

Kos leaned back. "Ladies before gentlemen. How about telling me about you first? Tell me, what do you want to accomplish in show business? You look like you have it pretty well put together—successful, young up-and-coming professional. Are you in college?"

There seemed a mocking note in his questions, but maybe she was mistaken. Her mind whizzed through answers she might use—all lies, of course—in the thirty seconds it took the busboy to refresh their water.

"Oh no. I was—majoring in drama. Then, Angel offered me the opportunity to join the troupe in L.A. and I couldn't pass it up. That's what Angel and I were talking about when I met you."

"What about your family?"

"Oh—I haven't lived with them in awhile. I have one sister who still lives at home."

"And where is that?"

This was getting worse. She was having a hard time remembering what she had already told him. This wasn't going as she planned. He grilled her as if she was on trial. *Just calm down, Jessica. You can handle this.*

Before she answered, their orders arrived. The fuss of the waiter setting down their plates, sprinkling pasta with parmesan, and refreshing the hot bread was the distraction she needed.

Later, over a cup of cappuccino, she asked, "Were you serious the other day about "seeing" me? I thought–" She took a deep breath. "I thought you liked me a lot. You seemed as if you wanted to kiss me before Angel walked in."

"I do like you, Jessica." He reached across the table and touched her hands. "You're very attractive."

He searched her eyes for a long time, and then looked away.

"Do you remember when I asked you how old you were and you said you were eighteen?"

Her heart thumped in her chest.

"Jess, I didn't believe you. Why are you lying? Are you in trouble?"

"I'm not lying—," she began. "—what makes you think I'm lying?" Her hands trembled and she placed them in her lap.

"Oh, give me a break, Jess. I'm not stupid. You're faking it—and not too well. Why is it so important that I think you're older?"

She felt the blood drain from her face, then heat with humiliation. With the realization that he had seen right through her lie, she became desperate. Genuine tears brimmed in her eyes.

She fingered the necklace she wore. "Please don't tell anyone this, will you? I'm so sorry I lied to you, but I *must get away.* I've wanted to be a singer and dancer like Angel since I was six years old. I can't wait five more years, which is what my parents want. I can't even wait two years until I'm eighteen. I *know* I can make it. Even with Angel backing me, there's no way my parents will agree to it—if I tell them. They don't care about my dreams or me. Oh, they notice me when I upset them or disturb their so-called reputation. My mom keeps telling me how stupid

I am to think I can make it in show business. This is my big chance." She pleaded, "You understand, don't you?"

"Maybe your mother is right. Do you have any idea how hard it is to go on the road? The routines take every drop of energy out of you. The competition out there is unbelievable. And the L.A. sharks will eat you alive and think nothing of it."

"But—but, I thought you cared about me enough to protect me and help me learn the routines faster so I can fit in right away. I've had jazz and done cheerleading routines for years. I'm strong. I can take it. I know I can."

"What do you know about me? For all you know I'm a serial killer. I'm telling you, Jess, you're walking right into danger."

"Kos, all I know is that I lo— care about you. Angel believes in me—enough to make me an offer. You two are my answer, my big break. Don't you see? I just can't let it go. Besides, you'll see. You'll learn to care about me. I may be young, but my feelings won't change. Don't you feel *something* for me?"

She leaned across the table and clutched his hands, choking back more tears.

He removed her hands. "Please. I don't mean to hurt you. You don't understand. It's *because* I care about you that I'm telling you these things. You don't even know *your own* mind yet. This isn't as simple as you think."

He looked away. "I care about you, but not in the way you're asking. There are important things you don't know."

Jess dabbed her eyes with her napkin, then found a tissue in her handbag and blew her nose. She felt insulted and hurt that he brushed her off when she had exposed her feelings.

Kos ran his fingers through his hair.

"Okay, listen to me, and hear me well, Jess. I'll go along with teaching you the routines, but you have to promise me you'll do what I say. You may not think so, but you're getting into a dangerous situation."

He continued, "Tell your parents about Angel's proposal, that you'll receive private tutoring in L.A. so you won't miss out on your classes, and that it's just a temporary situation to see what you want to do. If they agree and you can get away, come to the dance studio at nine Saturday night and I'll teach you the basic moves. I'll write down the address."

"Oh, Kos, that's beautiful. I'll be there. You'll be glad you did this."

"Promise me you'll clear it with your parents."

The waiter interrupted. "Will there be anything else, Sir?"

As Kos took care of the check, Jess looked at her watch and jumped up. "Omigosh. I have to go. I'm sorry I have to rush off, Kos, but I must be somewhere in fifteen minutes. See you Saturday."

She picked up her handbag and hurried out.

⌘　⌘　⌘

Kos watched her leave. It hadn't escaped his notice she ignored his request to tell her parents. He shook his head. *The dumb kid. She hasn't a clue of the danger she's putting herself into.* He wondered what made her so unhappy. Despite his better judgment, he knew he had to keep an eye on her from now on. She'll never know how lucky she was that she came to him instead of a predator, which, for all she knew, might be him. She was ripe for trouble.

Chapter 15

"Oh what a tangled web we weave..."

Jess sat in the middle of her bed. She imagined every detail of her meeting with Kos later that evening. Her thoughts brought a dreamy smile to her lips.

She had slept little last night, awakening long before anyone else in the house. Not even the rivers of rain sliding down her window dampened her anticipation. She considered this day as the dawning of a new life for her, although just another drizzly, dark November day to most. It wouldn't be too long before all things fell into place. *It won't be long until I'm out of here AND I'll be with him. He'll love me. I know I can make him love me.*

Yessir, it was a great day. She was off restriction—as if that hindered her—and Monica was off her back, happy as a kid in Disneyland because she'd made the cheerleading team. She learned fast—Jess had to give her that. It surprised her, too, that her self-righteous sister would stoop as low as blackmail.

"I bet she's pretty mad today. Her first practice cancelled because of the weather."

Her thoughts returned to Kos. She *knew* she would get him to pay attention to her as a woman—maybe tonight. She shivered.

A rap on her door startled her. Who else was awake?

She heard her mother's angry voice through the door. "Jessica Ann, come into the family room. Your father and I want to talk to you."

Uh-oh. Anytime Mom called her by her full name, there's trouble on the horizon. If her father waited, too, she stood little chance of winning him out of a bad mood this early in the morning. She rummaged in her closet for her flip-flops. There wasn't time to shower and dress.

Anne Nelson stared out the patio doors with her back to the rest of the family. Arms crossed, one foot tapped the tiled floor. Another sign, Jess noted, of her anger.

Eric leaned against the bar in the corner of the den and rotated his DAD coffee mug between his hands. He stared into the mug except for occasional glances at his wife.

Monica sat on the white bearskin rug, her shoulders hunched and her chin dragging the floor.

Jess slipped into the room, waiting for someone to break the silence. Her dad wore his plaid robe and striped pajamas, his thinning hair uncombed. Monica wore her Snoopy pajamas and slippers. Mom's sleepwear looked like she had stepped out of a thirties movie set. The hard set of her jaw and the frilly robe didn't match.

Her mother abruptly turned and walked toward her. Each footstep made Jess wince.

"Young lady, you've got yourself in quite a mess this time."

"Wha—"

"*Do–not–interrupt*." Her voice was soft, but lethal. "Your father and I had a very long talk with your principal yesterday, and she had surprising news. Out of the last two weeks, you've skipped classes seven times. She also said the attendance office had sent notes and left messages notifying us of your absences, to which we didn't respond because *we never received them*. According to school rules, she has no choice except suspending you for the rest of the school semester."

Jess felt sick. She looked at her dad for rescue. He wouldn't meet her eyes.

"Eric, you tell her about the humiliating rumors circulating the school about her. Everyone—the students, the teachers, and office staff—know. We'll never live down the disgrace." She sat on the sofa, massaging her temples.

Eric placed his cup on the bar and walked toward Jess, his expression stern. She thought she saw hurt and disappointment in his eyes, too. Something shriveled within her.

"Daddy," she pleaded.

"No, Jessica, this matter is too serious to allow you to talk me out of the decision your mother and I have reached. I take teen

157

gossip with a grain of salt, but when the talk reaches the ears of the school administration, I feel there must be some element of truth to it. Your habitual truancy is very disturbing to us. Lying is becoming a habit with you. Worse, your grades are dropping and you will not graduate with your class."

"Daddy, the rumors aren't true. Monica started them." She shot a vicious look at her sister, and then looked at her father. "And-and, I can bring my grades up. I promise."

"Monica has nothing to do with our decision today. Our decision is based on Ms. Sampson's and the school board's recommendations. We called Monica here because she withheld information from us and the school and covered up for you."

"Covered up," she screeched in amazement, and then lunged for Monica. Anne jumped from the sofa and grabbed Jessica's arm.

"How dare you scream at your father and attack your sister." She dropped her voice and said, "You've been nothing but a rebellious brat since you were six years old."

Eric loosened Anne's hold on Jess' arm and said, "Anne, back off. Control yourself. This isn't helping."

He turned to Jess, who sobbed and rubbed her reddened arm.

"You are still underage and under our care, and *we* make decisions about your life as long as you live in our house. Your mother and I decided we are enrolling you in a good private school where they specialize in counseling troubled teens. It is obvious you have problems, and we want to spare you a lot of unhappiness in the future."

"You're sending me to *reform* school? How can that spare unhappiness?" Her sobs came out in deep gulps.

"You're not going to reform school. Ms. Sampson suggested fine schools, with high academic standards, an excellent student body, and individual attention. They are not detention facilities, but they are boarding schools. She'll have more suggestions when we meet Monday morning. You are expected there, too."

"I won't go. You can't do this to me without even a warning."

"Oh yes we can, and we will," said Anne.

Jess couldn't believe the hatefulness of her mother, and, worse still, the betrayal of her father. She turned and fled from the room.

Locked in her room, Jess fell across her bed, sobbing. *They're sending me away. They're treating me like a criminal.* Sobs racked her in broken-hearted gulps.

Several minutes later, she quieted. She looked around her room, memorizing all of her prized possessions she must leave behind. She felt pushed from a sunny world of safety and security into a shadow-world of rejection and loneliness. Ten minutes ago, she couldn't wait to get out of the house, but cold reality shocked her. Like the view from the opposite end of a telescope, her plans and dreams became distant and small. This was huge.

Jess stood and squared her shoulders, making feverish plans. "Okay. If they want to get rid of me, I'll leave—tonight." She knew exactly where she would go. Instead of leaving with Angel in two weeks as planned, she'd run away with Kos. She would tell him tonight. *He loves me; I know he does. When I tell him what they're doing to me, he'll understand. He promised to protect me, didn't he?*

Jess ran to her closet and packed her workout bag with just a few more things until she could get some new clothes, sobbing the whole time. Unlocking her secret jewel chest, she took out some cash she had squirreled away from her allowance. Taking one last look, Jess slid out her window, pulling her bag after her and dropping it to the ground before she shimmied down the drainpipe.

The bus let her off a few minutes before nine. She tapped on the locked side door of the warehouse rehearsal studios owned by The Houston Ballet. The floodlights near the roof blazed down on her, and she felt conspicuous. No one approached her as she waited. A few minutes later, she heard the lock turn and the door pushed outward.

Kos welcomed her, already suited up in his rehearsal clothes.

"Did you have any trouble finding the place?" he asked as he locked the door behind them.

She shook her head. Her voice might tremble if she spoke. He led her down a dim hall. After entering a large, well-lit practice room, he pointed to a dressing room where she could change.

Inside the dressing room, she examined herself in the floor length mirror. Changed into her leotards, she felt proud her body was in great shape. She could compete with any woman in that department. She'd tell him about her plans when they finished rehearsal. By then, he'd have to agree.

One hour, two hours sped by. Kos was a patient and meticulous instructor. She discovered he choreographed all the routines, although he had been with the troupe for only a few months. The hard-driving practice music used was Angel's new release, and Jess was familiar with it. She had lost count how many times over the years she had danced along with Angel's music videos, envisioning herself on the screen, feeling the beat of the music coursing through her body. When the music ended, Kos went to the practice bars, retrieved a couple of towels, and tossed one to Jess.

They sat on the floor with their backs against the mirrors, toweling themselves off. As Jess dried herself, she felt his body heat, and her chest tightened. She couldn't figure out all of these strange but good feelings in her body whenever she was near him—or even thought about him. In fact, she couldn't stop thinking about him. Her obsession with him baffled her. It was as if she wanted to crawl inside his skin.

Kos stood and moved a few feet away from her. Had he read her thoughts? Embarrassment crawled up her neck. She stood, too, noticing the time on the wall clock across the room.

Almost midnight, and I still haven't told him. How am I going to explain so he will agree with me? Her plans didn't even make sense to her any more. Maybe she should think this through a little longer. She still had a chance to get back home without her folks discovering her absence.

She said, "I didn't realize how late it is. I don't even have time to change. I'll get my bag from the dressing room, and I must get home. I have a midnight curfew on weekends and I don't want to blow it with my parents." Another lie. It was as if she couldn't stop lying. What was happening to her?

When Jess returned, her hair combed and lipstick freshened, Kos said, "Wait here while I get the lights and turn in the key to the night deposit box. I'll drive you home."

She waited several feet away as Kos double-checked the lock.

Without warning, a large man wearing dark clothes emerged from a shadowy corner of the building, raised the butt of a pistol, and slammed it to the back of Kos's head. He crumpled to the ground. She opened her mouth to scream, but an arm encircled her in a chokehold and forced her backwards. The last thing she remembered was the pungent odor from the cold cloth placed firmly over her nose and mouth.

⌘   ⌘   ⌘

Kos opened his eyes; then closed them against the bright flashlight beam. He groaned, reached for the back of his head and felt a lump the size of a golf ball. Blood-matted hair covered the lump. He moved his arm and shielded his eyes.

"You can't sleep here. Move along or I'll pick you up for vagrancy."

A garbage can clattered. Kos looked around. He was in an alley propped between two garbage cans. *The attack came from behind and I didn't see it coming. I wasn't careful and they got to her.* Pain spiked through the back of his head when he struggled to his feet. Another groan slipped out.

"Look, Officer, I'm not a vagrant." He felt in his windbreaker pocket and then dropped his hand. His street clothes with his wallet were in his workout bag, now missing. He struck his forehead with the heel of his hand, realizing now Angel had set a trap for him, using the girl as bait. After all, it was her idea for him to instruct the teen. He could have kicked himself for believing her lies.

"Look, I'm a special agent with the FBI. My name is Karpati, Kostas Karpati. You can check with the Special Agent in Charge of the Houston Field Office."

The officer's partner joined them.

"You bet we will," said the first officer. "Rick, go back to the car and run a check on the guy. Should be no problem with a name like that."

He turned back to Kos. "Spell your name for my partner and turn around. Do you have any weapons on you?"

Kos shook his head. "Go ahead. Search me." The officer patted him down, which didn't take long because he just wore a windbreaker over his workout clothes. Rick returned and reported, "He's clean and his identity checks out."

"Can I go now? I've got to contact someone."

"Sure." In a marked change of attitude, the first officer asked, "Need a ride … need an ambulance? Looks like you've got a pretty nasty bump on your head."

"No, thanks, I'm okay. I'll take care of it later, but I need a ride and a quarter for a phone call. They knocked me out and stole my car keys and wallet.

The officers obliged.

He must check in right away. A simple search and the mastermind would know his identity. He had blown his cover. Kos felt lucky anyway, because if they already knew his identity, he'd be dead. This way, they will remove him from the assignment and reassign him to another case. This wasn't about him, though. Now it concerned a teen-age girl and her family. He wasn't sure how or when it happened, but the case was personal now. He knew he would break some rules, but he'd risk it to save Jessica's life.

During the drive, Kos had the rare opportunity to let his thoughts wander. He had failed his first undercover assignment. The more he thought about it, the more his head throbbed. His mind churned with self-blame and a sense of failure. These kinds of feelings had haunted him since his teen years in Bucharest. His sister, Catrine, and him, had barely survived the war in Romania. Catrine would be sixteen soon. Jess reminded him of Catrine. He had taken care of Catrine since their mother had abandoned them on the streets of Bucharest when he was thirteen and she was five. He didn't blame his mother. There was a terrible war going on. As a last resort, mothers often left their children on the city streets to spare them torture by the soldiers. Kos was old enough to understand he wouldn't see his mother again, because certain capture and death waited for her. Her abandonment was merciful. It was better for them if the police instead of the soldiers found them, because the authorities sent them to an orphanage—if they survived as street kids.

More bad memories came up. They were always hungry and cold; many times he worried that Catrine would die before he could return with food. Survival meant stealing and picking pockets, something of which he wasn't proud. Rumors about men roaming the streets abducting little girls for the sex trafficking business swept through the ranks of street-wise, homeless kids. Every moment he must leave Catrine alone was agony. A young girl or child who fell into the hands of these predators was a fate worse than death.

They lived like that for three long years.

A wave of homesickness came over him. He longed for the mountains of his country and wanted to see Catrine again. He was sixteen when he arrived in the United States. He had sailed when he knew his sister was safe at a Christian orphanage a few miles outside Bucharest. Bit by bit, he gained hope.

Kos fell back against the seat, his head pounding.

The squad car dropped him off at downtown police headquarters. As luck would have it, his cell phone had been in the stolen bag, too, but he found a pay phone near one of the bail bond businesses across the street from the station. He called his handling agent, who picked him up. As they drove to his apartment, he reported the events over the last twenty-four hours.

The next morning, Kos reported to the Special Agent in Charge of the field office for his formal debriefing and evaluation. In his own mind, he had committed the unthinkable for a law enforcement officer—getting involved with a suspect and blowing his cover.

SAIC Thompson arose and extended his hand to Kos when he arrived at his office. His Handling Agent and a recording secretary were the other persons present.

"Well, well, Agent Karpati, it's a pleasure to meet you face to face. So far, I've been acquainted just through your check-in calls. Sit down." Special Agent Thompson was a tall man, slim and fit and had a pleasant face that could blend into a crowd.

"Let's get started." Thompson sat down and took a few moments to review Kos's previous reports.

"I see here you've been undercover three months, but the investigation is incomplete. However, you did a good job collecting some key information about connections here in the States that we'll pass on to the people in London."

He glanced at the other Agent. "Jones, you turned in your report also?"

"Yes, sir."

"According to that report, 'Effective at approximately midnight, Agent Karpati was knocked unconscious by an unknown attacker, but whom Karpati suspects has connections with the organization under investigation, which attacker fled with his personal possessions. Those possessions included his ID as a special agent for the FBI, his cellular phone, and his wallet containing his counterfeit driver's license and his temporary address.'"

"Does that cover it, Karpati?"

"Yes sir." He quickly decided he'd omit his suspicions for now about Angel's part in the kidnapping.

Thompson studied Kos, assessing his mental status.

Kos sat still, keeping a poker face. Inside, he felt like a bug under a microscope.

At last, Thompson relaxed and wrote some notes on a yellow pad. Without looking up, he said, "Here are my recommendations: removal from the case; move out of your apartment; discontinue contact with any of the involved parties; report to Headquarters Support Division in Washington for a psychological examination; establish residence at another location; and report back to me in ten days for your next assignment. Good luck, Karpati."

After his debriefing, Kos took a cab and located his car where he had parked it before Jess's abduction. With relief, he found it intact at the same spot. He unlocked the Chevy with a spare key, and drove to his apartment on the west side of Houston.

He packed his few possessions, and, through the information from the bugged phone calls, found the exact location of the person at the delivery point in Europe. His search disclosed the location on a privately owned estate in a village southeast of London.

He flipped the cover of his cell phone and said, "Operator? Give me the number for British Airways reservation desk."

⌘　⌘　⌘

Angel tossed and turned. After awhile the drinks had put her to sleep, but, unchecked, the nightmares came:

Without opening her eyes, she feels his presence and reaches for the gun hidden under her pillow. Pa drinks every day now, and he hits harder. As he approaches, she awaits the familiar smell of liquor. She's confused. It isn't Pa. She opens her eyes. The intruder is a massive, hairy beast standing at the foot of her bed. It lunges and she gropes for the gun. She feels a jerk as her mind separates from her body and watches the events unfold beneath her. When the beast reaches her, it unscrews her head from her neck like a jar lid. Terror seizes her, but she feels no pain. She watches the creature step closer to her headless body, and then holds her head above him like a trophy.

She yells to her body, "Move! You're still *alive!" Shouting, yelling, screaming, but no sound comes. Her throat becomes raw and sore from her silent screams—the one sensation of pain she feels. She must—she must get the message through. Her brain directs,* "Move a toe, a finger, any muscle and run away."

"Oh what a tangled web we weave…"

She sees her chest moving up and down in gasps, expanding, and contracting beneath her nightgown. Time is running out and she will die if her head and body cannot connect soon. Relieved, she sees one finger move, and another, and then another. At last, everything connects. She runs outside, into the night, the echo of a gunshot and the smell of gun smoke trailing her.

Chapter 16

The Voodoo Priestess

Angel jerked awake. Tenacious wisps of the nightmare clung to her conscious mind before they drifted away. The darkened room and distorted shadows unnerved her. She needed light—any light. She found the illuminated hands of her clock. *Three in the morning.* Groping for the lamp switch, she turned it on. Gradually, the light calmed her, slowing her heartbeat and breathing.

However, once fully awake, pain exploded in her head and she felt a desperate thirst. She groaned, gripping her throbbing head. Crawling out of bed, she went into the bathroom for a glass of water. Staring at her pale face in the mirror, the memory of last night's overheard conversation crashed upon her. It occurred to her that maybe Philomena had laced her half-empty liquor bottle with one of her herb concoctions. That might explain her semi-conscious, paralyzed state during Philomena and A.P.'s visit.

The vein in her left temple pulsed. They had not acted aware she may be conscious, so the two talked about getting rid of her because, because—. In a rush, it all came back to her.

"Oh God—it can't be true. Philomena wouldn't kill me, would she?

Chills raised the hair on her arms, and she felt as if someone watched her. There was no sound and she couldn't see any light under the adjoining door connected to Philomena's apartment, but the feeling continued. A sudden reminder shook her senses. Philomena had developed the power of astral projection. Angel remembered her initial shock and fear when she discovered Philomena could detach her mind from her physical body and project it to another room or to the other side of the world if she chose.

Maybe that's why she has the feeling of another presence in the room. *Is she taking over my mind or casting a spell on me?* She dismissed the thought. Philomena's powers did not extend to mind reading. Some time ago, Angel had discovered that Philomena's claims as a psychic were trickery and merely keen powers of observation.

Tingles surged up her spine and her throat cut off her breath. A vision—or premonition—crossed her mind. A circle around a campfire, a stifling feeling, dark figures pressing closer, a sense of impending disaster.

Just as fast as the vision appeared, it disappeared. Normal awareness returned. She heard familiar sounds, like the whoosh of the air conditioner, distant sirens, and explosive wheezes of bus air brakes.

Before leaving the bathroom, she emptied a large, leaded glass vase for use as a weapon and checked the outer rooms of the suite for any signs of visitors—visible or invisible. Intuition told her the invisible entity that had watched her wasn't there any more. She sensed no one else in the room, so she walked to her closet, opened a hidden wall safe, and removed a spiral notebook. This secret notebook, her diary, recounted her thoughts, her desires. Off and on since she was thirteen, she had written there. Propping pillows behind her head, she placed the notebook on her knees, and wrote:

"Dear Diary: If there is a God like Darla said I need him now more than I ever have. Where are <u>you,</u> Darla? You are the one true friend I had in my life. You left and never said goodbye. What happened to you? Did you have to leave because Pa beat you, too?

"Well, Darla, if we ever meet again, you might want to know he's dead, so he'll never hurt anybody again.

"Do you remember, Darla, how we used to look at the stars and pick out one of our own? Now, I am that star I named Angel, and I have thousands of fans who scream and push and fight to see me. Yet they don't see the real me; they see the star. I need a friend, Darla. I need that wonderful God and Jesus you always talked about. They're going to kill me."

Why didn't Darla love her enough to stay? It hurt for a long time, but years ago, she had thought that being a celebrity with thousands of adoring fans would make her happy. How wrong she was. There was no happiness for her—

A soft tapping at the adjoining door broke into her thoughts. She stuffed her diary under the pillows and removed a book from the nightstand drawer.

"Come on in, Philomena—I'm just reading."

Angel opened the book and peered at the page, faking interest and deep concentration on the words. As if an apparition, Philomena appeared beside her bed. The lamp cast gold highlights on her deep amber skin, but hid her eyes in shadows. A braid hung down her back. Without her cheerful turban and flowered caftan, her presence seemed ominous. Her size and regal carriage left no doubt of her position as a high priestess of the voodoo arts, as she claimed. Angel, disturbed, sat higher in her bed and looked away. Tonight, she felt defenseless.

I'm not a thirteen-year-old kid any more, and I can't let her know she frightens me. Like driftwood, pieces of A. P. and Philomena's conversation surfaced. Their words drifted past, "… no good to us anymore. Get rid of her. Do whatever it takes."

Her heart knocked beneath her ribs, but knowing Philomena scented fear like a hound scented a raccoon, she dare not show fear. Yawning, Angel placed the book face down in her lap, stretching her arms above her head.

"Mmmm. Hi. You can't sleep either?"

Philomena shifted her head so that her eyes held Angel's, who felt the encroaching numbness of hypnosis.

Angel exerted all of her will power, breaking free of the mesmerizing gaze. Picking up the book, she tried reading.

With a shaky laugh she said, "Well, would you look at this. Upside down. Must be dull reading, huh?"

Philomena took the book out of her hands and placed it in the nightstand drawer. Sitting on the bed by Angel's feet, she spoke.

"You cannot hide anything from me. I see beyond walls and doors. I know many things you do not want me to know: your diary; your thoughts about the Christian God; this friend, Darla."

Angel pressed into the pillows, sliding her legs toward the edge of the bed. Her instinct told her to run. As if reading her thoughts, Philomena pinned Angel's legs to the bed.

"You have been promised to the sacred circle. You have had too much freedom already, and it's time you honor *our* gods."

Philomena's eyes sank deep into the darkness of her sockets. They changed, becoming opaque; blank, dead—a cobra before striking. Angel couldn't move. The priestess uttered incantations in an ancient tongue. Paralyzed and helpless, darkness invaded her mind and raided her will. It felt as if a hand had reached inside her head and squeezed her brain. Tighter and tighter. She had to scream, the pain was so intense. Then—the fist released her brain.

A spark flickered and steadied inside her head, pushing out the darkness. Scrambling out of bed, she bolted for the bathroom, slammed and locked the door. Before she fell on her knees and retched, Philomena, just outside the door, said, "Good night, Miss Angel-child. Sleep well. We have a long journey to make tomorrow."

Angel rested her head on the toilet seat. She shivered, but perspiration slid from her hairline and dripped from her chin. The heaving stopped, but waves of nausea attacked her stomach. When the raging battle within her digestive tract settled, she stood on shaky legs, walked to the washbasin, and splashed cold water on her face. She brushed her teeth, ridding her mouth of the vile aftertaste. Even so, the taste of bitterness lingered. After drying her face and neck with the terrycloth towel, she hugged it around her cold shoulders.

I must think of a way to get out of here and go to the police and tell them about the threats to kill me.

Unlocking the door with caution, she looked around her bedroom. She stood still, listening, drawing on her sixth sense. Once convinced she was alone, Angel rushed to her closet, dressed in jeans and shirt, removed a thousand dollars from her safe and stuffed the cash, her cell phone, and a few days' changes of clothes in her workout bag. She thought of her diary just before she left the suite, and ran back to her bedroom. She hurried through a search of bedcovers, quilts, under pillows, the mattress, and the bed. It was not there.

The precious book, now in the hands of the enemy, spurred her haste to get away. After checking the halls, she ran for the fire exit stairs, making sure she didn't let the heavy door slam. She heaved a sigh of relief when she reached the bottom and opened the door to the alley behind the hotel. *Now, if I can just get to the street before they notice I'm gone—*

An arm caught her in a stranglehold. She fought, kicking backward, and tried twisting free. Her foot connected with a shin; she heard a grunt of pain and his hold loosened for an instant. She prepared her body for a harder twist, and aimed her knee at her attacker's groin. Before she had good advantage, a chloroform-soaked cloth covered her mouth and nose. Seconds before she blacked out, Angel saw a black limousine turn in at end of the alley.

Chapter 17
Kidnapped

"Good. You're awake. Now we can have a little talk," said A.P.

Dazed, Angel shook her head and opened heavy eyelids. She looked at her surroundings. Peck sat behind his large, neat desk. She lay on the leather sofa opposite his desk. Two muscular men blocked the doors to the reception area and outer hall.

"What's–Where—?"

"Listen with close attention, because I'm going to say this once. If you refuse to cooperate–"

Every nerve in Angel's body jumped. Peck's tone, though soft, promised danger. She glanced at the two Mafia-type sentries at the doors. They were strangers to her. *God help me,* she prayed.

Peck nodded at the men and they stepped outside his office.

A few moments caught in his icy stare brought it all back— the terrifying supernatural encounter with Philomena, packing in a hurry, slipping out of the building via the fire stairways, the attack from behind.

"If you recall," he began, "I told you some time ago to select a young girl who is a–" He cleared his throat as if he didn't want the offensive word to pass his lips. "Umm—a girl with 'certain qualifications.' I didn't name a particular person, because I left that up to you. I requested a *pretense* you wanted her as a friend; I didn't ask you anything else, such as becoming her ally or devising your own plan to escape."

He leaned back, formed a steeple with his fingers, and continued, "I also instructed you to keep close attention on her for two weeks, reporting everything you had discovered about her to *me,* not make up your own plan and be stupid enough to tell someone else about it."

The word *stupid* struck her like a blow and she cringed. Oh yes, she had been stupid all right—stupid for trusting Philomena and A. P. all these years.

All of a sudden, Peck stood and the chair rebounded with a loud squeak. He strolled from behind the desk and picked up a good-sized jade figurine. He came closer, tossing and catching the figurine like a ball.

My God, he's going to kill me with it. She scooted to the corner of the sofa and drew her knees to her chest. Squeezing her eyes shut, she braced for the blow, hoping with crazy logic that if she couldn't see, it wasn't happening. When she didn't feel a hard blow, she opened her eyes with caution.

Peck hadn't moved. With a cold smile, he placed the figurine on a low table in front of the sofa. He seated himself in a leather armchair across from her and crossed his legs.

In a silky tone, A.P. said, "You didn't do as I told you. Now, you have jeopardized the plan even more with your drunken blackouts and other stupid tricks, like allowing some—" He thought a moment, searching for the right word. "—'Cocky' I believe is the American slang term—foreign dancer to draw the girl into *his* control. He wasn't part of the plan, hmmm? *You* decided so, because you liked wrapping yourself in your alcoholic cloud better."

She shook her head. "No, no, you're wrong. She—she slipped out of my hands and she lied to me. Besides, Kos doesn't know the *whole* plan—"

"And neither do you, my dear. So your best move is to be quiet from now on," Peck warned.

"Please, I can fix things—"

He held up his hand, stopping her. "Quiet. We have cancelled your London tour and arranged for a press conference once we reach Heathrow. Oh, by the way, we're leaving tonight. At the press conference, you announce that your physician has ordered your seclusion to an unnamed location for rest because of exhaustion. That's all you have to do. Simple enough?"

"Where am I going? Are you sending me somewhere to a sanitarium? I'm *not* an alcoholic—I can stop anytime I want to."

Peck brushed off her questions. "You know all you need to know for now." He glanced at his watch, rose and opened the office doors. "These gentlemen will take you—by force if necessary—to your limousine and you'll go without a word."

The taller man unbuttoned his jacket and opened one side, showing the gun within a shoulder holster. The other man grabbed her arm and jerked her to her feet.

"I'll wait for you at the airport," said A. P. "Necessary arrangements, clothing, news media, publicity releases, and so forth, have been taken care of by myself or Philomena. All you must do is smile for the photographers and look exhausted."

He murmured instructions to the armed man, who nodded. As Angel passed, he said, "Oh yes, one more thing. We have a brief stop along the way to pick up another passenger."

In spite of the threats, she had to ask, "Who are you talking about? Philomena's been in this all along, hasn't she? I heard both of you scheming against me the other night. She's doing horrible things to me with her spells and drugs and herbs."

Except for another warning glance, Angel's accusation left no impression on him. He said as he glanced at his watch, "Hmmm. Oh yes, Philomena. About now, she's getting the other passenger ready. That's enough of your questions." He waved the men on.

Inside the limousine, Angel thought fast. One thug drove and the other sat across from her, picking his teeth and watching her behind his sunglasses. She couldn't see his eyes, but she was sure they weren't friendly. She clamped her lips, but her teeth chattered anyway. If they hadn't ambushed her, she would have had a chance. In her heart, Angel refused to behave like a victim.

I will not be afraid of the gorilla with the gun and sunglasses anymore. I can out-think him. He follows A.P.'s orders, and A.P. wouldn't dare kill me—I'm too valuable alive, she reasoned. Hadn't she been in dangerous situations most of her life?

Darla entered her thoughts like a soothing balm. She wished she could time-travel back to those few good years when her big sister-friend had been in her life. She recalled the Sunday mornings while Pa had slept off Saturday night. On sunny Sundays, Darla and she sneaked to the woods at the edge of town. Stretching out beneath the trees, they took turns reading from Darla's old Bible.

"This is God's Book and this beautiful spot is His house of worship," Darla had told her.

Something Darla had read from that Bible popped into her head. Something Jesus had told his disciples when he sent them into the towns to preach, cast out demons, and heal the sick. He warned them that people would try harming them, or even kill them, when they went out in the world preaching about him, and they should be– it was something about snakes and doves. Then it came to her. *"Be as shrewd as snakes and innocent as doves."*

Angel wasted no more time reminiscing. Right now, she must think of a way of getting out of this and tell the police before it was too late. She could do it. She *would* escape.

183

⌘　⌘　⌘

Jess hadn't felt this awful in her life. She opened her eyes, realizing she was on a carpeted floor bound and gagged. She opened her mouth, but couldn't speak. Her bound feet and hands prevented movement. She wiggled into a sitting position and looked around her. Where was she? Something seemed a bit familiar about the room. She had been here before. Then, it came to her. This was Angel's suite, but how did she get here? She saw a phone and scooted toward it. She would call 9-1-1 using her nose if she had to.

She reached the low table and, after several tries, pushed the phone to the floor. She bent, straining toward the buttons, but large brown hands replaced the receiver and placed the phone on the table. She glimpsed sizeable bare feet beneath a bright yellow and brown print skirt. She looked up at the tallest, biggest woman she had ever seen, who wore a yellow turban, increasing her height by four inches.

The woman reached down and tore the tape from Jess' mouth. The sudden sting brought tears of pain to her eyes. Jess scooted backwards. *Who is this person? What will she do to me?* Questions scrambled across her mind.

The stranger picked her up like a farmhand picking up a bag of seed and tossed her on the sofa.

"Please untie me," she pleaded.

"And let you run away, little sister? Uh-uh. You goin' to take a long trip, and we take no chances."

The events before she lost consciousness came back to her.

"Where's Kos," she stammered.

"Oh. You mean that dancer? Don' worry. He's alive, but prob'ly has a ver' sore head."

"Who are you? What do you want with me?"

"I'm Philomena. That's all you need to know. No last name, address, or anything else, little sister."

There was a knock at the door. Philomena paused on her way, and turned to Jess. Her eyes gleamed with excitement. "You have been chosen, little one. You don't know how much the gods bless you by this choice."

Two men entered the room. One carried a large duffle bag.

Weak and drained, stark terror overtook her when they came toward her with the empty duffle bag. From behind, someone covered her mouth with duct tape before she could scream.

⌘　⌘　⌘

The limousine slowed and stopped. Angel's guard straightened, drew his gun and pointed it at her head. For the first time, he spoke. "If you don't want to get shot, don't make a move." She believed him and didn't move.

The door opened and two men tossed a squirming duffle bag at her feet. In the thirty seconds they had the door open, she glimpsed their location and recognized the back alley of her hotel.

"Okay Al, here's the other package to deliver to the airport," said one of the men.

The door slammed and the car moved into the early morning traffic. *All those cars—even police officers—on the road. I wish I could think of some way to get their attention without alerting the bodyguard.* However, a loaded gun pointed at her head and the dark tint of the windows prevented any way of signaling for help.

Once on the toll road to the airport, Al holstered his gun and opened the duffle bag. The squirming occupant poked out her head and maneuvered her hog-tied body into a sitting position. Angel's heart sank when she looked into the wide, terrified eyes of Jessica Ann Nelson. She looked away, but not soon enough to miss the heartbreak in Jess's expression.

Chapter 18

Terror

Al ripped the tape from Jess's mouth. She didn't flinch, still smarting from the emotional pain of Angel's betrayal.

"Angel?"

Angel turned her head away. Jess stared at her idol's profile. *She acts as if she had never seen me before.* Jess searched the star's face, looking for a trace of recognition, or some compassion. Anguish, hot and searing, burned in her chest. What had she done that deserved betrayal?

"Shut up or I'll shove you back in the bag," the man called Al said to her.

Jess shut up. The cords cut into her ankles and wrists if she moved. She looked at the big man, terrified by his threats. He removed his sunglasses, showing vicious, deep-set brown eyes. A lightning-bolt scar, carved from cheekbone to jaw, arced the right side of his face.

Jess closed her eyes. All of it was like a scene from a bad movie. *This isn't happening; I'll open my eyes, and wake up in my room.*

"Al, leave her alone," Angel pleaded. "She's just a scared kid who knows nothing—"

"—you shut your mouth, or I'll shut it permanently. Understand?" He drew the gun from inside his jacket and pointed it once again toward Angel's head.

Staring at the glinting barrel of the gun pointed at Angel, Jess now understood the truth. *So, they kidnapped Angel, too. Why? Where were they taking them?*

After a frightening ride in tense, electric silence, the car slowed and stopped. Someone opened the door and the deafening roar of jet engines shattered the silence inside the insulated limousine. Blinded, tied, and now deafened by the jet noise, Jess felt herself hoisted and slung over Al's shoulder. Difficulty breathing, choking because of the smell of jet fuel, and terrified, she squirmed and struggled, screaming as loud as she could through the thick tape and heavy canvas bag. Before long, she stopped struggling. If any sound came through at all, no one could hear above the jets anyway. The cords, tied by someone who must be an expert with knots, tightened with movement. She bounced against Al's back on the bumpy climb to the plane's cabin, each bounce increasing the pain in her bound ankles and wrists. The din muted once they entered the plane and closed the heavy door. Al walked a few steps and dropped her onto the floor without opening the bag. Bright red stars flashed when her head struck something hard.

Moments later, Jess heard the cabin door open, and Angel's voice screeching, "A.P., you'll never get away with this." Captor and captive struggled, punctuated by gasps and grunts.

The sounds of struggling stopped. Angel taunted through gasps, "The FBI starts looking for missing kids right away. Have you thought of that?"

"Shut up you bloody bi— Ye-owww! You bit me," Peck yelled.

"You may get away with hiding me for awhile, but when the law puts a few things together, they'll look for me, too."

Jess heard the thud of bodies falling and Angel's screams. Peck's curses and grunts of pain showed she fought hard. The struggle ended with the sound of fist hitting flesh, Angel's sigh, and then silence. Inside the duffle bag, Jess didn't move, pretending unconsciousness. Peck approached and placed Angel's body onto the seat above her head. The outer door opened and slammed, leaving them alone.

Jess wriggled her way over to Angel and butted her head against her legs but failed rousing her. She gave up and slumped against the seat.

⌘　⌘　⌘

Angel moaned and opened her eyes. Testing her jaw, she opened and closed her mouth, then winced as she touched it with her fingers. Sitting up, she saw Jess helpless in the duffle bag on the floor. She melted. The poor girl was in terrible danger through no fault of her own. She whispered, "Jess, just hang in there. I'll think of something. I promise."

The outer door slammed and the engines roared and vibrated the cabin as the plane rolled out for takeoff.

Once airborne, Peck walked back to them, opened the bag, unbound Jess's arms and legs, and removed the tape and blindfold. She straightened and blinked, adjusting her eyes to her surroundings. She looked down at the deep red marks embedding her wrists and ankles. She rubbed and flexed them, easing the throbbing pain.

Standing above her, Peck said, "You might as well find a seat and relax. We'll be in the air for a long time." She refused his offered hand and scrambled to her weak legs under her own power, collapsing into the seat across the aisle from Angel.

Shrugging, he said, "Suit yourself. I won't hurt you if there's no trouble. But if you try anything, I will restrain you again."

⌘　⌘　⌘

During the long flight, Angel and Jess had the freedom of moving about the cabin; they even helped themselves to a light meal heated in the microwave oven. For short periods, Peck wasn't close enough to overhear their conversations, so Angel explained to Jess in whispers what had happened. She comforted and reassured her co-captive, forgetting her own fear.

However, when their journey ended twelve hours later, another criminal-looking type entered the cabin, blindfolded, bound and gagged Jess again, and left the plane with her. They had separated them, which, Angel thought, was not too promising when she came up with an escape plan later.

When her turn came to exit the plane, with A.P. close behind her holding a revolver, Angel smiled and waved to a small group of reporters and fans waiting for her at London's Heathrow Airport. Once on the tarmac, Peck concealed the revolver and stayed close enough to hold it to her back while they disembarked and moved through the crowd. Upon arrival at a private door to the building, he pocketed the gun and moved aside when security police escorted her to a private lounge.

When she arrived in the lounge, Philomena waited.

"Ah, Miss Angel," Philomena said. "So good to see you. Did you have a nice trip?" She wore an expensive dark blue suit, tailored for her full figure. She had braided her hair, the braid coiled and nested beneath a stylish felt hat.

What a striking change from the same voodoo priestess who invoked curses on her less than twenty-four hours ago. It was common that Philomena accompanied her on concert tours, but she hadn't expected her under these circumstances.

"My, my, lil' girl, you look all beat up. We get you freshened up ver' quick for your fans."

Philomena motioned away others crowding the room, grasped Angel's arm, and guided her to the quiet luxury of the powder room.

Once alone, Philomena dropped the act. She removed her hat and jacket and peered at Angel's tired face. She grabbed Angel's chin and lifted her face to the light. The right side of her jaw showed swelling and an ugly bruise.

"Hmmm. Looks like you made the mistake of puttin' up a fight. Tsk, tsk. Did no good, did it? Well, we'll take care of all that with makeup, a different hairstyle, and a change of clothes. Gotta look nice for the photographers." Humming to herself, she set out a makeup case and began working.

Flashbulb fireworks and reporters shouting questions greeted her when she entered the pressroom. A.P. stood behind her, his hand in his jacket pocket with his revolver. She dropped thoughts of an outcry or escape attempt. *I must find out where they've taken Jess so I don't endanger her life, too.*

Movie star style, Angel flashed brilliant smiles, turning her best angles for the cameras. Her blonde hair, styled loose and casual, covered her jaw line. Her fair skin contrasted with dark smudges of exhaustion beneath her eyes, confirming to the casual eye her fragile state of health. Altogether, a convincing performance and Philomena's makeup skills rendered her last-minute cancellation of the concert plausible to the fan magazine columnists and reporters—at least for the moment. Fifteen minutes later, she ended the press conference.

Terror

Because of Philomena's hot tea dosed with potent herbs and forty-eight hours without sleep, Angel fell asleep as soon as she entered the back seat of the Rolls provided for her transportation.

Another Rolls-Royce followed them, holding Jess, also unconscious.

Chapter 19
Missing

The following morning in the Nelson household, something startled Monica awake from a deep sleep. She had no idea what brought her awake. She sat up, rubbing her eyes. It was morning already. She still had her clothes on and it took her a moment to figure out why. Awareness dawned that she must have fallen asleep waiting for Jess. She owed her an apology for tattling and lying.

The previous evening, Monica had knocked on Jess's door, but there was no response. Usually, when Jess was mad or unhappy, she climbed out the window and went off somewhere. Jess thought no one knew about her secret escape route, but Monica knew. Most of the time she didn't care what time her sister sneaked back in, but she felt partly responsible for the extreme punishment decided by her parents. She didn't want Jess sent away.

Oh God, forgive me. I didn't tell mom or dad all of the truth and I wanted to get back at Jess for what she did at our party.

Monica glanced at her watch. *Eight o'clock.* How late did Jess come in? She had last checked at two in the morning. Slapping water on her face, she wrapped herself in her robe and tapped on her sister's door. After knocking several times without a response—usually a shoe thrown at the door—alarms went off in her head. Feeling under the carpet for a bobby pin she hid there, she picked the lock of her sister's bedroom door. Empty. She hadn't slept in her bed, either.

She saw Jess's wrinkled jeans and shirt tossed on the bed, a sign she had been home at some time since she last saw her. One wedgie platform shoe rested on its side by her bed. The other was in the corner. This isn't right, she thought. Her scalp prickled in fear.

She searched Jess's closet for a clue. Her leather jacket and workout bag were missing, a few of her clothes, and the door to her locked box was ajar and emptied. *She didn't really run away, did she? Oh, no, no, no. This is worse than I thought.*

Monica flew downstairs, yelling all the way.

"Mom, Dad. Something's happened to Jessica."

⌘　⌘　⌘

That afternoon, Eric, his voice low and tight, spoke on the phone to an investigator with the Sheriff's department. "Listen,

Sir, my sixteen-year-old daughter is missing, and you haven't done anything. If you can't do anything, get me someone who can." He paused, listening for a few minutes before angry words spilled out, his control destroyed.

"I don't care what your staffing problems are. My daughter may be hurt and her life may be in danger right now—she *did not* run away from home. If you won't do something *now*, I will." He jammed the 'end call' button and slammed the phone into its cradle.

Anne and Monica stared, shocked by his uncharacteristic outburst. Anne walked to him and touched his shoulder. He turned his back, shrugging off her hand. Unyielding, he didn't speak.

Anne returned her arm to her side and stepped back. "Calm down, Eric. This will get us nowhere, and we must have the law's cooperation in finding Jessica before–" Her voice trailed off.

Eric turned to her, his face drawn and beaten, and said, "Before they discover her body. That's what you were going to say, wasn't it?"

"No, oh no. I meant— Oh, I don't know what I meant." She sank to the sofa, covering her face.

Monica rushed to Anne. She hadn't seen her mom so heartbroken before. She put her arms around her, sobbing, too. "Mom, mom. Please don't cry. She'll come home. She's just mad and trying to make you guys worry."

Eric turned and walked toward the door. He looked stooped and older.

"Dad. Where are you going?"

Eric kept walking. Without turning, he lifted his arm, halting her questions. "I just need time alone to think," he mumbled.

Fear, like cold feet, crept up Monica's spine. Her parents had changed and her world became topsy-turvy overnight. Mom, normally strong and confident, became a helpless mess. She had never seen her dad explode in anger, either. She prayed, *Oh, God, please make Jessica all right. It's my fault for not telling everything I knew in time.*

Jessica didn't come home the second night either. Eric had gathered his thoughts and took charge, called and contacted all of the law enforcement agencies and volunteer search organizations he could think of or find on the internet. Soon, flyers were out, search teams organized, news media contacted showing Jess's picture. Investigators, organizers, advisors, and friends crowded their home all day and night. No one in the Nelson household slept. Eric kept vigil over the phones. No one in the house made or received outside calls. While he kept watch, he made dozens of calls on his cell to relatives, her friends, and finally, the hospitals and city morgue.

The Sheriff's Department investigator showed up; crime scene investigators searched their home; another team of investigators questioned each family member in separate rooms. They took many notes but answered few questions. When Monica's turn for questioning came, an attractive blonde woman approached her. She introduced herself as Detective Amanda Duff.

Monica forced a polite smile, twisting her cold fingers in her lap.

"Did your sister have a boyfriend, or boyfriends, who may help with some information?"

"Well, you see, Jess and I didn't confide in each other. We had a big fight the day before, and, and —" Monica covered her face with both hands and sobbed in remorse.

"It's my entire fault. You see, Mom and Dad planned on sending her to boarding school and she was furious—"

"Yes, your parents mentioned that and it's been noted," said Detective Duff. "Back to my question: did you know about any boyfriends, did your sister break up with anyone, or was there another boyfriend who had a grudge or threatened her? Did she talk about any specific boy bothering her or stalking her?"

Monica accepted a Kleenex the detective handed her and dried her eyes. "I did overhear her talking real low to someone she called *Hoss* or *Ross* or *Koss* a couple of times. Before that, she dated someone named Eddie, but she didn't want our parents to know about it. She didn't want to talk to me about it, either, accusing me of being snoopy and, as usual, her accusation started another fight between us."

Monica dabbed tears with a damp tissue.

"Wait—I do remember something strange. A couple weeks ago, she came home very late with her top torn and her hair all messed up. She looked like she'd been crying. She-she wouldn't tell me anything, though."

"Do you know where she went that night, or who she was with?"

"Well, she was dating Eddie at the time." Shame filled Monica when she recalled the dirty rumor she had planted at school. She avoided the detective's eyes.

Detective Duff didn't press for an answer.

Yet, Monica's fear for Jess motivated her confession. "I started a rumor at school that she was pregnant and blamed the rumor on her best friend, Pam. My sister and I had a big fight about that just before she went missing."

The detective continued jotting notes. After Detective Duff finished writing, she said, "Do you have a last name and an address for this friend, Pam, or Eddie?"

Monica sighed in relief after the detective let her go. She hadn't realized how burdened she felt about her act of revenge.

When she returned to her room, she looked up and prayed, "God, please don't punish Jess for what I did."

Someone organized a search party the next day. Monica watched live coverage on TV. A human chain, shoulder to shoulder, searched every inch of open fields. Knowing the searchers looked for her twin sister was strange. Seeing the posters with a face identical to hers pierced her soul.

The Highway Department posted Amber Alerts, and her parents appeared on TV news reports pleading for any information about her whereabouts. Soon, the quiet Sugar Land neighborhood filled with curious crowds, the press, TV mobile units, and concerned neighbors. The Nelson's home became a command center for the FBI and Fort Bend County Sheriff's task force — monitoring and screening phone calls, interviewing family, friends and neighbors.

Three days passed without contact from Jess or anyone who had spotted her. The reporters thinned and moved on after two days, but heartbreaking crank calls got through and a steady stream of traffic passed by, as if sightseeing neighborhood Christmas decorations. Eric, Anne, and Monica withdrew into their own thoughts and 'what ifs.'

The family unit crumbled and collapsed in their separateness. It had been another dismal day of waiting, hoping, but not wanting, a telephone call. Unable to bear another moment of excruciating waiting, Monica went to Jess's room where her sister had been — alive and exasperating.

She walked down the hall and saw the door ajar, and, involuntarily, her heart jumped. Her anticipation died when, instead of Jess, she saw two men jotting notes in spiral notebooks, opening drawers, and turning over the mattress.

Rage raced through her and she shoved the door open, shouting, "Get out of my sister's room." She rushed to one man and jerked an article of Jess's clothing out of his hand, sobbing and hitting the startled investigator on his arm. The other man came behind her, pinning her arms to her side.

"Whoa, young lady. We're FBI and your father gave us permission to search your sister's room. It's part of our investigation."

Monica went limp in his grip, but she couldn't stop sobbing.

"You–you act like she's dead," she wailed.

Anne appeared at the door, with red-rimmed eyes and a worried frown. "What's all the commotion?" Monica freed herself and ran to her mother.

A brief explanation from the agent satisfied Anne; she put her arm around Monica's shoulders and led her to her room. Eric arrived, too, checking out the shouting. He shut the door while Anne urged Monica into bed, shaking out a capsule from a bottle she drew from her pocket.

"Eric, will you please get her a glass of water from her bathroom?"

"God, where are you–do you even care," Monica moaned. Anne bent and gathered Monica into her arms. She rocked her, whispering, "It's okay, sh-sh-sh, hush, it's okay." Eric set the glass of water on the nightstand and dropped to his knees, embracing his wife and daughter.

The sedative and comfort helped Monica sleep well that night. At dawn, she jerked awake. She heard her sister's voice, "Pray, Monica, I want to come home." She sat upright. *Jess is alive. That's her voice. I would know it anywhere.* The clarity and closeness of her twin's voice seemed so real she peered through the pre-dawn dimness searching for her.

Gradually, Monica realized Jess's words were part of a dream, but calm and peace came to her. When she had said her prayers as a little girl, she knew God took care of things while she slept. She snuggled close to the pillows and fell asleep again.

An edgy peace settled on the household. Hope warmed the family and brought them together, although the sheriff's office or the FBI hadn't mentioned any new developments.

That night, Eric, Anne, and Monica heard people crowding their front yard.

"Did you hear that? It sounds like singing." Monica came downstairs, her head cocked, listening.

"I heard *something,*" said Anne. "It's coming from the front yard. I hope the news reporters haven't come back."

Eric entered from the kitchen. His brown eyes—once merry and laughing—were dull and lifeless.

He led the way to the big window overlooking the front yard and drew the drapes. Pinpoints of candlelight pierced the darkness, covering their front lawn into the street. The people behind the candles sang hymns in low voices. In the candlelight glow haloing their faces, Monica recognized her youth pastor and some members of her youth group. Her heart wrenched when the group sang, "*It is well, it is well with my soul.*" Monica grasped her parents' hands and sang along.

Chapter 20

The Earl

Across the Atlantic on his estate in the English countryside, The Honorable Cecil Beckingham, Earl of Wortham, took the letter from the silver tray held by his butler. Whenever the envelope sealed with the family crest arrived each month, he expected a sizeable check. The check, written by his aunt, the Duchess of Hedington, had arrived at the same time of the month for nine years. He recognized the spidery handwriting of the family matriarch on the envelope. Cecil had never liked the woman, and it irritated him that she ruled the dispensation of money he had inherited.

Searching for the check, he shook out the folds of the two-page letter. There was no check. Perhaps the letter explained.

My dear nephew:
It pains me to inform you the funds delivered to you since your twenty-first birthday ceased on your thirtieth

birthday, in accordance with your father's will. As you know, a stipulation required your marriage and the birth of an heir by your thirtieth birthday. Unfortunately, neither has occurred. The remainder of the funds in the trust reverts to the family. Of course, the land and your dwellings shall remain in your hands until your death or the sale of the property, or portion thereof. I trust that you have applied the funds over the years to the maintenance and repair of your inheritance. Your land alone is valuable for use by the timber-producing industry. That alone, I am sure, is sufficient for maintenance of your family home.

I extend belated happy birthday greetings.
Fondly,

Cecil flung the letter to the floor and shoved off the objects atop his desk. How *dare* they withhold money to which he had a right?

He regained control of his emotions and tapped his fingers on the polished desktop, thinking matters through. An idea came to him, but it involved premature contact with his detestable cousin, expected in two weeks. Cecil shook off his distaste and reached for his cell phone. He must make a long distance call. His plan would work if handled well—

A tap at the door interrupted him. Annoyed, Cecil said, "Come in."

"Mr. Arnold Peck is waiting to see you, Milord," announced Charles.

The Earl raised his eyebrows in surprise. *What an uncanny stroke of luck, and I saved a few pounds for an international call as well.*

"Send him in, Charles—but have him wait a few moments."

He tidied his desk. In view of the sudden downturn of his financial future, Peck's unexpected visit afforded the opportunity to tell his wealthy outlaw cousin he had reconsidered taking part in a moneymaking scheme he had proposed last spring.

Charles served tea and they relaxed—at least the Earl did. He never missed tea, and visitors must join him whether they wished or not. Neither man spoke as they sipped their tea. Logs snapped and popped in the freshly lit fire and filled the silence.

The Earl took a sip of his tea. "It's delicious, isn't it? I have it shipped from a plantation in the Chinese interior."

Peck shifted in his chair. His jaw muscle twitched and his crossed right leg bounced in a rhythm of impatience.

Cecil looked at the bouncing leg, amused by his cousin's discomfort. At last, he replaced his cup and saucer on the tray and summoned Charles to remove the tea service.

Settling back in his chair, he said, "Well, well, well. What brings you earlier than I expected, Arnold?"

"I had an unexpected bit of business in London, and drove here to speak with you about a crucial change in our mutual plans—"

Peck looked toward the library doors and leaned closer, lowering his voice. "Look, is there some place where we can speak that's private?"

Cecil rose from the chair, walked to his desk, and withdrew a set of keys. "Yes. In fact, *I* have something to discuss with *you,* which is confidential, too. Follow me."

The two men made their way to the lower floor of the unoccupied east wing of the castle. It was damp and chilly in the small, out-of-the-way room that the Earl used for his hideaway office, but in a short time, warmed by a blazing fire.

Standing before the fireplace warming his hands, Peck began. "It has turned out that my biggest moneymaking star, Angel, entertains plans to run away, which must be stopped at all costs. Complicating matters is her heavy drinking and refusal to stop. She is embarrassing and rebellious and her performances are affected. So, I'm losing money because of her."

Peck turned away from the fireplace and stared at Cecil. "I want Angel to withdraw from the public eye for a while. You will hold her here until I get back with you. I'll have air-tight plans in place for her future by then. The woman, Philomena, Angel's guardian, has other plans for her that does not interfere in my original business with you. Without family ties, her disappearance won't be investigated right away."

With a casual air, Peck inspected his fingernails before he added, "But, you understand, we must carry out the plan by force, meaning it's important that she's secured in a place she cannot escape and cannot get messages to the outside. I've found she can be quite devious and scheming at times."

Cecil walked to the small desk and sat on its edge. He pursed his lips, as if in deep thought, but avoided eye contact with Peck. He didn't care for his cousin's intense, probing stare, and he didn't trust him. There was something missing in his story. He would wait.

Slipping off the desk corner, Cecil confronted Peck. "So, what do you require of me that changes our original plan?"

"The other girl you asked for is with her and it's important you keep them separated. I don't want them to get their heads together and plan an escape scheme. It's none of my business what you do with the other girl. I'm simply delivering what you paid for."

"Hmmm, I see. You understand, of course, that your addition of another *guest* requires extra accommodations, which are expensive, but I'm willing to take care of it if you do something for me."

Peck glared at the Earl. "You're joking. How many rooms do you have in this pile of rocks? And—you want to bargain with me? Do not insult my intelligence. Will you or will you not hold Angel for me?"

"Agreed. Shall we shake on it, or *must* you have it in writing?" The Earl's question held a mocking note, and Peck's color darkened.

"Now, now. Temper, temper," Cecil warned. "In any event, my proposal is this: I have reconsidered the offer you proposed several months ago."

Apparently seizing the opportunity to win a skirmish in their verbal warfare, Peck sneered, "Well, well. So you've reconsidered, have you? I'm surprised you'll soil your lily-white, *aristocratic* hands"

Hiding his thoughts, the Earl walked to the fireplace and studied the flames. Arnold's insult was demeaning and he loathed the situation his family had forced on him. Dealing with his despised cousin in matters of money sickened him. Arnold ranked so far beneath him that he would not even qualify as one of his servants. Ah, but he was wealthy and his financial sources discreet. Cecil realized he must lay his plans with care and set aside personal sensibilities. Arnold's availability and his attractive offer would provide the money he needed for satisfaction of his—appetites. Appetites misunderstood by legitimate sources like banks and such. He had a special purpose for the estate, and that purpose required secrecy and his absolute control.

He faced Peck. "You mentioned a 'contact' interested in young girls—for a certain price. I will provide a steady supply for quite a long time—at the right price, you understand. With your contacts and my supply, we can do business."

"Of course. I never retract on an offer, and I gave you my word as a *gentleman* I would take care of your request in all its stipulations."

Another insult intended to sting. Nevertheless, Cecil extended a limp hand. "Gentleman to gentleman, shall we shake hands on it now and settle the paperwork later? When you arrive with the girls, everything will be ready here. We will keep in touch, but with caution. Now—let us leave here. When we arrive at the drawing room, I'll have Charles show you out."

Chapter 21

The Tower Prison

Jess awakened bound, gagged, and blindfolded. This time it seemed there was a significant change about everything—temperature, noise, and surroundings. It felt like a cave. Her sense of smell reacted to the foul stench in the damp room. She held her breath as long as she could spare her nauseated stomach more distress by taking light, short breaths until she became acclimated to the odor. She remembered a long plane trip and a bumpy ride inside a large bag, but nothing after that. The blindfold was so tight she couldn't open her eyes. The truth hit her with a hard blow. The cold, the cords around her wrists and ankles, the rough stone floor were authentic.

"Ah, yer comin' to." She heard a coarse male voice and couldn't detect his position, but scented stale tobacco and rotten teeth, which put his face too close to hers. She scooted away, bearing painful scrapes to her flesh from the floor's pebbly stones.

"It's about time ya' woke up, luv. Welcome to jolly old England. Me name's Gordy."

Gordy ripped away the tape and blindfold. She blinked, and saw his grinning face above hers. He had a sharp, narrow nose and prominent cigarette-stained teeth. He reminded her of a huge rodent.

He removed the cords from her ankles and she scrambled to her feet. Her weakened legs wobbled but held her upright. Gordy walked a few feet away, speaking into a cell phone as he walked. He finished his call, ground out his cigarette on the stone floor, and reached for something at the beltline of his pants.

The dim light bulb suspended from the ceiling gleamed on the blade of a knife. She kept her eyes on the knife, asking, "What do you people want with me?" Her teeth chattered with fright and cold. "Let me go home, please."

Where was her daddy? He had always been there when she needed him.

"Keep yer mouth shut, luv. I'm takin' ya to see someone." She froze at the touch of the knife at her throat.

⌘　⌘　⌘

Outside, the other luxury car arrived and waited at the gate to a circular driveway leading to the manor house. Surrounding the estate, fifteen-foot-high iron gates secured the property. The gates parted, rumbling on pulleys. The noise awakened Angel from her drug-induced sleep. The Rolls passed a turret-shaped gatehouse, and the man inside tipped his cap to the driver. Angel pressed her face to the window, cupping her hands around her temples to see well. Straight ahead, the silhouette of a massive castle floated above the ground mist. Here and there small squares of light indicated occupancy. As the car rounded a curve, a grove of trees blocked her view, but, moving on, the structure emerged bit by bit.

Where are we? This isn't London. She had fallen asleep as soon as they took the road from Heathrow, but she expected a short trip to a hotel. She sank back in her seat, baffled.

Peck pinned her arms behind her and put cuffs on her wrists.

"These are to keep you out of trouble. It's no use struggling. We're too far away to call for help, so don't attempt escape. Keep such ideas out of that scheming little mind of yours," he said.

Angel looked around her. Her heart sank. "Where's Jessica?"

"She's in good hands."

His arrogant smile increased her alarm for her friend.

She remembered her promise that she would figure something out. She said a silent prayer. *Oh, God, help her. It's my fault she's involved in this.* Her soul shriveled with guilt as she remembered the darker reason she had chosen Jess. She sent another prayer pleading with God that they hadn't killed her.

Peck opened the door, helped her out of the car, and hustled her up stone steps leading to tall, hand-carved oak doors. Inside, a tall man dressed in a black tuxedo led them through a long, wide hall. Closed doors on both sides led to other rooms. During the short walk, Angel memorized her surroundings and tucked the information away in her mind. Old wealth and nobility soaked the mansion. She took in the centerpiece of the grand hall—the sweeping staircase—with hand-carved, ivory-colored banisters. A deep burgundy carpet covered the circular stairway. Polished suits of armor lined the hall. Stern faces in family portraits painted centuries ago stared down on any visitor who passed beneath them. Angel shivered.

They arrived at twin doors beyond the staircase, and the man in black opened the doors, stepped aside, and gestured them inside. The servant left, closing the doors behind him. Angel stumbled across the threshold when A.P. shoved her.

From a dim area of the drawing room, a man said, "My, my, if it isn't my *dear* cousin Arnie. And who accompanies you, Cousin?"

Peck pushed Angel ahead of him. A slender young man arose from a brass-studded leather chair and walked toward the two.

Peck frowned. "Don't call me Arnie."

"Whatever you wish, dear cousin," he said. "Why don't you and your guest make yourselves comfortable before the fireplace and I'll join you for tea."

Angel repressed a shudder. She had heard that voice before. This was the phone contact.

The Earl looked at Angel, and addressed his cousin, "Oh please, Arnold, are the handcuffs necessary? She's not a common felon. Uncuff her hands."

Angel wondered why he treated her as if a guest rather than a prisoner—for that's what she was despite the luxurious surroundings. She supposed the charade gave the slender, short man a feeling of superiority, but she would go along with it. She lifted her chin, looked straight ahead, and floated into the room in her best royal style, praying he didn't see the rapid pulse at her throat. Predators smelled fear.

Peck removed the cuffs and said, "I'll leave now, Cecil, but let's meet later and conclude the other business matter you and I discussed earlier."

Without taking his eyes off Angel, the Earl nodded.

Angel walked serenely to the brocade wing chair near the fireplace when every nerve in her body screamed, 'run.' She could play *Charades,* too. The Earl appeared amused by her bluff, approaching her in an exaggerated courtly manner, bowing and reaching for her hand. He assisted her to her seat.

She inspected his face as he drew closer. He had pale, unblemished skin and well-defined, delicate features, a well-groomed moustache, and thinning blonde hair combed over a bald patch. She restrained a shudder when his moist, smooth lips pressed the back of her hand.

"My dear, you are more beautiful than you appear on the screen. I'm so sorry you've had 'to go into seclusion' for awhile—that is what you announced at your press conference, isn't it?"

He seated himself in the chair opposite her, crossing one leg over the other. His arctic blue eyes studied her, assessing her. She compressed her lips to stop her teeth from chattering, a dead giveaway for the cold fear inside her.

Nodding with satisfaction, the Earl continued, "Unfortunately, I cannot tell you our location—not that you'd tell anyone, hmmm? This is one of the many crumbling castles across the British Empire, but I've become rather attached to it because I grew up here. It's not much, but it is home." He swept a limp hand around the room.

Angel smiled politely. Behind her smile she thought, *this place is a fortress stuck in the middle of nowhere. How will we get out of here?* She guessed they had brought Jess here, too, separating them on purpose. This man had as much warmth as a shark. She took a deep breath and counted to five in her head. She couldn't go on with this cat and mouse game any longer.

Gathering courage, she said, "Look, sir or lord or baron, whoever you are, you can't keep me here against my will—I'll contact the American Embassy —" Even to her own ears, her threat sounded weak.

"What do you intend to do, my dear, walk back to London." the Earl asked. "Unless you sprout wings, you cannot escape from the tower, which, by the way, is your new home. We don't have telephones in every room; in fact, there are no telephone land lines to this remote area." He took a cell phone from his coat pocket and flipped it open with his thumb. "Nevertheless, we're not so medieval that we do not have any modern methods of communication." He replaced the phone and called his servant by pressing a small button on a nearby table.

"However—" He cleared his throat. "— your accommodations are much more comfortable than our dungeon, where we keep uncooperative guests. Yes, indeed, my ancestral home has a dungeon, too. Not to worry, though, you won't be there or in the tower for long—until you're needed."

"Needed–what do you mean?" Her voice trembled.

A rap on the entry doors interrupted.

"Come in."

"You called for me, your Lordship?"

"Take the young lady to her quarters, Charles. She's very tired."

⌘　⌘　⌘

Back in the States, Kos didn't have a problem booking the next flight from Houston to London. During the flight, he pieced things together. He concluded that if Jessica and Angel came up missing at the same time under suspicious circumstances, Angel was a victim rather than a collaborator. Discreetly showing his ID to an attendant, he discovered that no person or persons fitting either girl's description, accompanied or unaccompanied, were on the passenger lists for flights to London within the last forty-eight hours. Then, he recalled that on tours Angel, the musicians, and dancers traveled in her private jet.

When Kos arrived in London the next day, he visited an airport newsstand and saw a photo of Angel on the front page of a magazine. In each shot, A.P. stood just inches away from her — a tip-off he held her against her will. In addition, he knew her statements to the press about a rest were lies. However, where was he taking the girls? A few questions to airport employees obtained all of the answers he needed and then he was on his way in a rental car to southern Kent County.

When the journey ended at the nearest village to the estate, Kos found lodgings at a boarding house. He presented himself as an American student on his first trip abroad. A few visits to the village pub and a few inquiries resulted in a job as a janitor and groundskeeper a few days a week at the estate. He familiarized himself with the castle layout and the grounds. Avoiding suspicion, he studied the area at night and on his days off.

One afternoon, while reconnoitering the unoccupied living quarters in the east wing, Kos heard the voices of two men approaching the basement. Ducking behind a heavy beam in the unused laundry room, he watched the men approach a locked steel door across a narrow hallway. He recognized Angel's agent, Peck. The thinner, blond man must be the owner. The owner unlocked the door by using a combination. In the few seconds the door remained open while they had their backs turned, he darted inside. Crouching behind a sofa in the darkest corner of the room, he watched them approach the fireplace.

So far, so good, he thought. His dark clothes hid him, too, but he touched the bulge of the holstered pistol beneath his jacket for reassurance.

The blonde, younger man stood with his back to the fireplace and placed his hands in his pockets. "My, my, how clever of you, Cousin Arnold. How did *you* win such a prize," he asked.

His mouth twitched with a sarcastic smile. "The last I heard she was in on the scheme. Is she mine or just for you, hmmm?"

"Let's say she's no longer of use to me, Cecil. The single matter for you to be concerned about now is that she accidentally disappears—permanently," said Peck.

"Why would you want to get rid of your meal ticket? I thought you said her guardian had plans for her."

"That's *my* concern. I've thought it over and decided to change the plans. At the last minute, the woman crossed me. Y*our* concern is Angel. All you must do is hold her for a little while until I return and dispose of her. I assure you no one is looking for her now."

"Hmmm. I hope you're right. I can't afford nosy reporters, family, or police tracing either girl here. I have a family name and reputation to uphold. I *will not*, under any circumstances, allow a drop of scandal or publicity to touch us."

"Do you think I'm fool? *I* have a legitimate business to protect."

Turning, the Earl walked toward the safe. "Very well, let's get on with the final details."

"—Yes, yes, get on with it. I don't have time for tea parties." Peck looked at his watch. "Where is the list and the pickup spot?"

"Of course." Cecil paused before opening the safe. "Oh, yes. Refresh my memory. In your initial invitation to participate in your scheme, your—uh—contacts offered one hundred thousand — per piece, wasn't it?"

Peck's face reddened and veins bulged at his temples. "*Per shipment,* you vile piece of scum."

"My, my. It's unfortunate we didn't have a witness or papers drawn up at that time so we can be sure. I'm terribly sorry about the misunderstanding. Hmmm, too bad. I have five more girls ready at this moment. You have my assurance they are flawless. Two are seven and nine and quite lovely. I happen to know the younger ones are worth a fortune to traffickers, likely *more* than a hundred thousand."

Peck seethed—his body stiffened like a pit bull poised for attack.

The Earl stroked his moustache. "Tell you what, I'm feeling a bit generous, and I'm willing to throw in the three older ones for two hundred thousand."

As Kos listened to the perverse haggling, he felt sickened. His emotions struggled with his training and self-discipline. He wanted to put a bullet into both of their heads.

They were no good to him dead. He had to get his hands on the videos and papers in that safe and locate Angel and Jessica hidden somewhere in the castle.

Chapter 22

Trapped

Angel's mind raced, searching for ideas as she followed the butler, Charles, out of the drawing room. *Maybe this man will help—he looks harmless; maybe there's a sympathetic maid; maybe I can climb out a window and get help from neighbors.* She couldn't think straight and abandoned plans for immediate escape, confident she'd think of something later.

Charles led her along a hall connecting the east wing to the west wing and then through a deserted kitchen. They stopped at a narrow, circular staircase, the stone steps concave from hundreds of years of human steps. She hung back hoping for an escape opportunity, but Charles held one candle lighting the way ahead, and, as they spiraled upward darkness closed in behind her. She had no choice; she followed. He unlocked a sturdy oak door decorated with an ancient iron latch and brass studs and then lit the candles placed around the room.

While he started a fire, Angel looked around, her heart sinking. A freezing, high-ceilinged room was her quarters. One arched window, barred, provided natural light.

After starting a fire, Charles said, "Come."

Angel felt as if she had stepped into a storybook or a movie set. Charles's deep bass voice, skeletal frame dressed in black and his creepy behavior reminded her of a character in a 'B' horror movie.

Charles pointed to a cubbyhole next to a small table with fresh towels, a basin, and a pitcher. "This is the W.C., and your bed is turned down and ready." He pointed to a high, canopied bed.

Gesturing to the wall adjacent to the fireplace, he said, "There is fresh clothing in the wardroom over there."

Charles turned to leave.

"Wait– How long will I be here? What do they want with me? Why are they treating me this way?" Hot tears streaked down her cheeks.

Charles stopped and looked at her. For an instant, compassion flickered in his deep-set eyes. The expression disappeared and he walked out. Seconds later, she heard the key latch the door.

Silence engulfed the room. Shadows cast on the wall from the fire danced in tempo with wind gusts whipping at the window. Angel fell on her knees and prayed. Several minutes later, she felt calmer. "There must be an escape route. These old castles have secret doors and tunnels."

Trapped

She had discovered this for herself while on location in Scotland a couple of years ago. Haunted castles fascinated her, and the locals answered her questions with enthusiasm. Even the family in residence had taken her on a private tour. It had all been quite amusing then and provided distraction from the hours alone in her hotel suite. She was not amused now.

Angel searched the room. She had seen the momentary softening in the butler's eyes before he left. Maybe she could get his help after all.

While she searched, tapping sections of the wall and lifting rugs, she heard the key inserted into the lock. She ran to the bed and tugged the covers to her chin.

Her visitor wasn't Charles or another servant as she expected. The master of the castle, himself, walked in.

The Earl looked at the bedcovers clutched to her chin and said, "You needn't be concerned about showing your body. I have no interest in your person except its value to others."

"What are you talking about? What's going on?" Ransom? Or? Horror crawled up her spine. *No. It can't be what I suspected they had planned for Jessica. That's too evil for civilized people to do.*

He reached over and jerked the covers out of her hands. She scrambled to the other side of the bed on all fours. She slid to the floor searching for a weapon. Though slender, he had a wiry strength and he caught one arm and twisted it behind her back. She fell to her knees in front of the fireplace. With her free arm, she groped for the poker but it clattered to the stone hearth. He kicked it out of her reach. She reached into the fireplace, grabbed a handful of hot embers and threw them at his face as hard as she could.

With a howl of pain, he let go of her arm and pawed at his eyes. She lunged for the poker, sucking her breath through her teeth in agony when her raw palm gripped the poker. Despite the searing pain, she stood and raised the poker above her head—

The door opened and two men rushed in, shouting, "Stop, stop!" One grabbed the poker out of her hand, intensifying the pain unbearably. A heavy, hard object hit her on the head, and she collapsed, unconscious.

⌘　⌘　⌘

In a basement room, a guard had Jess in a stranglehold, a knife held near her throat. She dared not struggle when he told her to walk to the tower stairs. His stinking, sweating body choked her as much as his arm around her neck and dirty hand covering her mouth. She felt a prick and the flow of warm blood at the hollow of her throat before he slipped the knife into the belt of his jeans. The same butler who had admitted them when they had arrived waited for them at the foot of the tower stairs. When they reached him, he led them to a small door next to the stairs, unlocked it, and pulled the chain of a bare light bulb. In the dim light, Jess saw a compact storeroom stocked with canned and packaged goods. Once inside with the door shut, her captor released his grip and pushed her forward. She fell to the rough cement floor, scraping her knees and hands. Terrified, Jess rubbed her bleeding knees. Freed from the guard's hand over her mouth, she screamed, "Help—anyone. Help!"

The butler spoke. "Screaming won't help. You are in a place that has been a fortress against invaders for seven hundred years. The walls are eight feet thick."

In that moment, Jess's traumatized, tormented mind separated from her body. She observed herself from a position three feet above her, weightless in a cocoon. The butler spoke to her guard, his mouth moving, but producing no sound. She thought it peculiar seeing everything as if on a TV screen with the mute button on. From her suspended place, she felt safe. She heard a whisper. *It will be okay, Jess. We'll find you.* It sounded like Monica.

She observed herself follow the butler down stairs hidden behind a tall cupboard. Then, she fainted.

The strong smell of incense brought her to consciousness. Stinging smoke drifted into her nose and throat, bringing a fit of coughing. Strong arms helped her to her feet and steadied her. Dazed, she glanced at her surroundings. Black candles held by hooded and robed people lit the subterranean room. Chanting, they formed a circle around a pentagram painted on the floor. A hooded figure broke from the circle and led her to the center. The faces beneath the hoods looked like skulls in the candlelight. Shaking, Jess fell to her knees.

The droning chant ceased and a male voice spoke.

"You are here for a sacred purpose, but you must be inspected for proof of your purity."

Inspected, sacred–what do they mean? The pieces fell into place. That must be why Angel had asked if she was a virgin. She sucked in a deep breath. No—they wouldn't—they can't. People don't do things like this except in horror movies—

The speaker broke into her terrified thoughts. "First, you must be quieted so you will cooperate."

Another person lifted her to her feet and bound her hands. Another walked toward her, holding a cup of steaming liquid.

"No—no! I won't drink that. Let me go–Oh, God help me."

Jess thrashed her head back and forth. She screamed when another from the circle jerked her head back by her hair, immobilizing her. She tasted bitter liquid dribbling down her throat and seeping out the corners of her mouth. He forced the contents into her mouth until the drug weakened, then stopped her struggling. She sobbed, pleading, "God–help–me–" Darkness again conquered her consciousness.

Light stabbed Jess's eyes. Immersed in feathery softness, she asked herself, *Am I in heaven; did they kill me?* Moments later, she realized the softness wasn't a cloud, but a down coverlet on a four-poster bed. Opposite, a large fireplace with glowing logs warmed the room. The noon sun shone through a high, arched window. She fingered the high-necked flannel nightgown she wore, wondering what had happened to her clothes. A velvet robe, with matching slippers placed beneath, hung on a wooden valet. She shivered despite the cheerful fire and luxury. The events of the night before washed over her with the force of a tsunami.

The chants, circle around the pentagram, drugged tea gave her a surrealistic picture, like a Salvador Dali painting. Her throat tightened as she looked around her surroundings. She was in a prison—a luxurious one—but still a prison. Hundreds of questions tumbled in her mind. What did they do to her mind and body? How could she explain the horrifying ritual she recalled? Drug-induced hallucinations? What did they mean she had to pass a test of purity? Was Angel in on this? No, she remembered the day before on the airplane. Angel was a prisoner, too. She had a faint memory of one normal event in the last few days— standing outside the dance studio waiting for Kos. Nothing but insanity after that.

Questions continued plaguing her, and a memory surfaced about an awful thing that had happened at school last year. There had been rumors at school about a group of high school kids into cults and witchcraft, a teacher mixed up in it and later fired, a student named Jon who committed suicide, and police asking questions. The awful discoveries brought gossip and excitement among the students for a few weeks. Parents and teachers said nothing about it—very hush-hush—and the rumors died. Word got around that Jon's suicide was an accidental drug overdose. She had been acquainted with Jon and remembered him as a happy-go-lucky kid and very popular. Suicide hadn't made sense to her.

Anyway, none of it had involved her or her friends. She didn't do drugs and never intended to. She had thought she was too smart to mess up her mind, and nothing like that could happen to her. But, here she was. She couldn't breathe, her heart knocked beneath her ribs, and a continual chill reminded her of the truth.

Voices outside the door broke into her thoughts. She drew the covers to her neck and shrank into the pillows. Looking at the unyielding, flat blue sky through the high window she whispered, "Oh, God, what do I do now?" The brilliant sun and shimmering, perfect sky had disappeared. Somewhere, she knew, God existed. Today, he seemed light years away. She waited, light-headed with paralyzing fear.

Chapter 23

Escape Plans

Angel opened her eyes to the cheerful command, "All right, luv, ye must get up."

The brogue belonged to a plump woman with white hair. Glasses perched atop her nose beneath bright blue eyes.

Angel pushed herself upright. Burning pain covered her hand.

"Ow-w-w-w!" She fell back on the pillows and felt sharp soreness on the right side of her skull. She probed her sore head with her fingertips and felt a large lump.

"Here, here, now. Ye've had a nasty bump and burn. Let me 'elp ye."

The fairy godmother-type person placed her hands under her shoulders and adjusted the pillows. While she searched her mind about what had happened, the woman introduced herself.

"Me name is Mrs. O'Reilly, and I'm here to t'help ye ready yerself for a visit with 'Is Lordship in 'is study.

"Please help me—" She caught movement out of the corner of her eye. Charles waited in the shadows. He must be the watchdog for the Earl. Help from that source wouldn't happen.

The hairs on the back of her neck stiffened. Regardless of Mrs. O'Reilly's deceptive appearance, she lodged in the enemy's camp.

Angel decided submission seemed best for now. Her bumps and burns from last night proved aggression failed and she was outnumbered. She'd think of something else. She had learned that a clear mind made an excellent weapon. She had been in danger before, but these new dangers and intimidating prison fortress shook her confidence. Panic edged closer, but she had one more weapon. She prayed for a miracle.

Thirty minutes later, her charge fed and dressed, Mrs. O'Reilly bobbed her head to Charles and departed.

After handcuffing her, Charles nudged Angel out the door. She busied her mind by familiarizing herself with every detail possible, searching for exits. They arrived at a door located below ground level. The Earl waited outside the door. Bandages covered one side of his face, leaving one good eye glaring at her. A tiny smile lifted one side of her mouth. *Good. I hope I blinded him.*

His good eye glittered with anger and she stopped smiling. After Charles left, he keyed the combination for the door and pushed her inside, gesturing her to a chair. She looked around, surprised because of the room's small size and plain furnishings—not the ordinary idea of a nobleman's study. The room contained a scarred and scratched roll top desk, a couple of shabby wingback chairs, and a large cabinet. An old-fashioned safe squatted in the opposite corner.

He looked at the swath of bandages covering her hand and head and said, "So, you're a fighter, are you? Well my little wildcat, you'll regret using your claws on me."

He settled himself in the chair opposite her and examined his fingernails. The silence stretched, oppressive and sinister. She wanted to scream. She focused on the crackling flames in the fireplace, the single source of light in the gloomy room.

He finished his fingernail inspection and looked at her. "Since you *insist* on knowing my plans, I'll show them to you now. You'll have several hours to digest them. I will also show you the plans for your little teen-age friend."

Rising, he strolled to the safe; and, without turning or pausing said, "Oh, by the way, midnight tomorrow is the 'witching hour' so to speak." He chuckled at his twisted joke. "After that you begin your new adventure."

Squatting before the safe, he turned the combination lock. Whether he didn't cover the lock on purpose or by carelessness, Angel didn't know. She suspected he did it as a taunt. Even so, she wouldn't let an opportunity pass. She had a gift for fast memorization and excellent distance vision. If she leaned forward a bit, she had an unblocked view. He withdrew a videotape in an unlabeled cartridge and inserted it into the VCR slot. She already had the combination memorized.

He pressed the remote and the screen flickered to life. Images sharpened, showing a clearing lit by campfire, bordered by thick woods. The bottom of the screen showed a recording date of midnight, one year ago. A procession of robed and hooded people, faces hidden, circled the fire and chanted—low at first, and then louder. The chanters moved away from the campfire to a stone altar. Behind the altar, other hooded figures erected a tall object, the details hidden by shadows. Louder and louder, they chanted unknown words increasing to a climatic frenzied outcry—

Angel closed her eyes and turned her head away from the screen. She wanted to cover her ears, too, but cuffs bound her hands. The Earl stepped behind her chair and, with an iron grip, forced her face toward the screen. She twisted and struggled, squeezing her eyes tighter. His grip tightened with every movement, like a python.

"Oh, no, my pet, you must watch and you must listen."

A scream clawed its way up her throat. His implacable cruelty chilled her, and she knew she must not relax her vigilance. The noise of the updraft from a freshly lit bonfire drew her eyes to the screen. She gasped. The screen showed an inverted cross engulfed in flames. Mesmerized by the horror, she fastened her eyes on the screen.

A slender, teenage boy robed in white processed to the altar. He slowly raised and outspread his arms. His face covered the screen in a close-up, and his drug-dilated eyes stared rapturously at the inverted cross. *This—this person with his hands on me is a man with wealth and power in league with the devil himself—*

Her soul cried out, *Oh God, oh Jesus. Help us. He will kill us.* Nausea surged to her throat.

The chanting stopped. Just a chorus of crickets broke the midnight silence. A barefoot girl—by her shape and size about nine or ten—walked into the clearing. She wore a filmy white gown and a coronet of flowers crowned her dark hair. When she reached the boy, she fell to her knees and bent her face to the ground—

The images on the screen shrank into a pinpoint of light.

"There's more, but it seems you get the message now," he said.

A bitter taste of bile flooded her mouth seconds before she lost her breakfast.

Disgust curled his lips, and he summoned a servant for a clean up. Angel retched miserably.

The Earl left the room and waited in the hall, holding the door open. He held the doorknob with one hand and pinched his nostrils closed with the other. The janitor arrived and began cleaning. Once Angel's heaving intestines quieted, she watched the janitor work. A glimmer of recognition pricked her mind. He was young, with a dark complexion and thick, black hair. He wore baggy coveralls. She noticed well-built shoulders and arms, which triggered memories of dancing with those arms around her. She bit her lips, stifling a gasp. *It can't be. How did he find out where we are?* Hope lifted her despair.

The man noticed her moment of recognition and shook his head a tiny bit, his eyes shifting toward the door.

"Hurry along, won't you," demanded the Earl to the servant. He said to Angel, "If Charles doesn't come soon, I'll deliver you to your room myself, and it won't be pleasant." He stepped out into the hall peering at the top of the basement stairs.

The delay provided precious minutes, and Angel nodded toward the safe and signed the combination she had memorized. He nodded his head and finished mopping. Seconds later, angered and impatient, the Earl charged toward the entrance, colliding with the janitor. The door slammed and locked the Earl outside, enraging him more. "You bloody dolt. Why don't you watch where you're going?"

The young man bobbed and touched his forehead in apology, and the irritated nobleman waved him away as if he was an annoying gnat. The Earl went inside for Angel, pushed her into the hall, and locked the door. Alert dark eyes watched and memorized the combination before he hurried away.

In the tower room fifteen minutes later, Angel shook with agitation. The events in the past hour unnerved her, but help had arrived. She hoped Kos could get them out of here within the window of two or three hours before they took them away. She *must* find Jessica before tonight. But, how? She'd think of one thing and discard it, and another as too impossible. There was one thing left for her to do. She fell on her knees beside the bed and bowed her head.

"Oh Lord," she prayed, "Please bring a miracle. I don't know much about you except for what Darla told me when I was a kid and by what you've already done to help me." She knew she didn't deserve any of God's attention because of the life she had led, but deep in her heart she ached for something she didn't have, she couldn't buy, she couldn't find by traveling all over the world. Tears slipped from her eyes. She wanted love. Even now, thinking about her past, every nerve crawled with shame.

Despite the chilly room, sweat trickled beneath her armpits and beaded her hairline. She removed her woolen robe and tossed it on the bed. She paced the small room, but her thoughts became more confused. Barefoot and wearing a thin cotton nightgown, it wasn't long before she shivered with the cold. She glanced at the fireplace, noticing the fire had burned down to embers. Picking up the poker, she bent closer, moving the logs for a better fire. An odd sight drew her eyes to the wardrobe to her right. She moved closer and noticed someone had moved the massive piece several inches away from the wall.

"That's funny," she murmured, "Why was it moved?" She squeezed in the opening, her hands flat against the back, pushing with all her weight. After several tries, the wardrobe moved, revealing more of the wall space. She squatted and twisted the handle of a door, which opened to an old-fashioned dumbwaiter. A small person might fit—even two small persons—turning it into a mini-elevator. She peered into the opening, seeing that the thick rope pulleys descended into the darkness to the bottom—the kitchen area. She withdrew her head when the pulleys moved and squealed. The dumbwaiter stopped at the floor below her.

⌘　⌘　⌘

Jessica's attendant entered, placing the key in the pocket of her apron. She was a square-jawed woman with a face chiseled from granite. She wore a kerchief around her head, her apron covering a print dress. Sensible black oxfords and woolen socks completed her apparel. She built a fire, brought hot food on a tray, and supplied fresh linens and clothing. Conversation consisted of commands issued in guttural monosyllables in a German accent. "Eat. Sit here. Will come tomorrow."

Initially, Jess's foggy thoughts couldn't distinguish between her dreams and reality. She tasted bitter herbs in her tea and occasionally saw the uncommunicative German woman inject a needle into her arm. She lost perception of time and place.

Nevertheless, she gathered her strength after her attendant left, got out of bed, and dumped the tea into the fire. She was too weak to fight the sturdy woman's injections into her arm. Occasionally, though, she had lucid periods.

In the lapses of clarity, the danger of her situation bore down on her. She had many questions. Where did they take Angel? Did they kill her? Did they intend killing *her?* When? Looking around her room, she felt like she had fallen from a time machine into the dark ages.

Escape Plans

That evening, the woman, who had identified herself as Mrs. Schmidt, took her tray and dishes to the dumbwaiter, grunted *Auf Wiedersehen,* and left. Even her fearsome keeper provided human company, and she hated the moments when she left and locked her in with the ghosts.

Yes, she now knew medieval ghosts haunted the room. They came with moans and whispers; she felt bone-chilling cold spots, sensations of touches—like fingers—on her cheek. Horror forced her eyes closed and fastened her to the bed so she couldn't move. The ghostly visits pushed her to the far edge of sanity. Extreme exhaustion and the rosy tint of dawn on the clouds brought sleep.

After Mrs. Schmidt had locked the door, Jess waited for her spectral visitors but after an hour, they had not come.

"Where are you? Don't torture me any more," she shouted to the empty room. "Either come or stay away forever."

After several minutes of silence, she relaxed and settled under the covers.

⌘   ⌘   ⌘

In the room above the sleeping Jess, Angel had discovered the dumbwaiter hidden behind the chest. When the pulleys ceased moving at the floor below, she watched and listened as a square of light and the sound of clinking dishes followed. Before she closed the door, she heard a heavily accented female voice speak to a person in the room. She caught a snippet of her sentence—that was enough. Jessica was in the room below hers. She closed the door and pushed the wardrobe against the wall. Her first thought thanked God for providing a miracle. Although she hadn't figured a way to contact Jess yet, she knew God would provide a way. They now had their escape route. Amazement brought her to her knees. "Thank you, thank you, and thank you." Wonderful. The Big God of the Universe had heard her.

Now that they had a way out, they needed a plan. How will she let Jess know? Once they escaped from the tower prison, they would find Kos—or, he'd show up. "If he got in he must know how to get out of this place," she muttered.

She checked both rooms again for hidden passages. Nothing. She started when a log fragment fell off the grate. The fireplace. Of course. The rooms must have a common chimney. Sound would carry through it—wouldn't it?

Her heart raced as she dashed to the hearth and removed the screen. She took the shovel and spread the ashes, killing the last embers. Bracing herself with her left arm, she reached inside, searching for the damper. A small object slipped from beneath her right hand. A cell phone. She picked it up and turned it on. The bars on the face showed strong reception. It must have fallen from one of the men's pocket in her scuffle with the Earl last night.

Escape Plans

She raised her eyes skyward, thanking God. Another miracle. She turned it off and dropped it into her robe pocket. God had provided all she needed for now. She had nothing more to do but wait until everyone went to sleep.

Chapter 24

Escape

Later that night, Angel crept out of bed and retrieved a candle. Her hand shook as she lit the candle. She judged about four hours had passed, which would put the time about ten-thirty. She had an hour and a half to execute her plan. Cupping her hand around the flame, she tiptoed to the cold fireplace. She approached the opening and the candle sputtered—nearly extinguished by the wind gusts funneling through the chimney.

Angel took a deep breath and said a quick prayer. She set the candle on the mantle, kneeled and thrust her head as far as she could into the fireplace. She tried a loud stage whisper first: "Jess. It's Angel. Come—to—the—fireplace." She hoped no one but Jess occupied the room.

⌘ ⌘ ⌘

A sound jerked Jessica from the precipice of deep sleep. *Oh, no. The ghosts came back.* She listened a moment and realized the sounds came from the fireplace. The flames flickered and died. *It must be just the wind coming through the chimney, I hope.* Fully awake, she jumped out of bed and ran to the hearth. The stone floor felt like blocks of ice on her bare feet.

Listening intently, Jess heard someone call her name. Sticking her head far into the fireplace, she heard, "Jess, it's Angel. Are you there?" Angel was alive. In an instant, lightheartedness and hope replaced Jess's despair.

Her voice shook as she replied, "Angel, is it really you?"

"Jess, are you hurt?"

"No—just bruises and scrapes. They're putting drugs into my tea and forcing a needle in my arm, but I get rid of the tea when my attendant leaves—Angel, are they going to kill us?"

"Not if I can help it."

Angel's determination reassured Jess.

"We don't have much time, because I know they're coming for us in about an hour. Listen—I think there's a way we can get out of here now. Do you see the door about the size of a cupboard door to the right of the fireplace?"

"Yes, I see it."

"Okay. Open it and you'll see pulleys attached to a dumbwaiter. I'm bringing it up to my room above yours and I'll lower myself to your room. Luckily, I found a cell phone that still has a signal. I'll bring it with me and give it to you, but we'll have to wait until we get out before we try getting through to your folks. That will be the quickest way we can get the law here. The FBI probably has a tap on your parents' phone."

Jess's heart missed a few beats in nervous excitement.

"Great. "But, can the dumbwaiter hold both of us?"

"Yeah. It's roomy—as big as a refrigerator crate. Are you ready?"

"Give me a few minutes to find my clothes."

Before she rushed to the wardrobe to change, Jess looked out at the sprinkle of stars framed by the tiny window and prayed, "Please, God. Make it all work."

While she dressed, she heard rapping from the fireplace— Angel's signal.

Grabbing her jacket, Jess ran to the dumbwaiter door. She opened it and watched the crate-sized metal box ascending with noisy creaks and groans. It was sizeable and sturdy, the opening protected by a sliding metal door. She heard Angel above her entering the carrier. A minute later, she faced Angel for the first time in three days.

"Hurry. Get in. It's a tight squeeze but we'll make it." Angel reached through the opening and caught Jess's hand. Jess squatted and balanced on the ledge, rolling her body inside. With knees drawn up, sitting side by side, they fit with inches to spare. Angel reached outside and tugged on the steel cable. Their descent began.

For caution's sake, they spoke in whispers. It took about five minutes to reach the bottom. Before reaching bottom, Angel closed the metal door of the dumbwaiter. They listened for several seconds, making sure the room was empty, and moved through the kitchen and laundry room. Angel pointed to a bolted door. Unbolting the door, she pushed it wide enough for them to get through.

Jess squeezed through and dashed for cover to a tall hedge a few feet away. Angel prepared for her sprint to the hedge, but a strong arm clamped around her neck and dragged her inside. She squealed with surprise, squirming and struggling, but his hold tightened.

"I'm not going to hurt you, Angel—stop struggling," he whispered.

"Kos." When she quieted, he released her and turned her around to face him, raising a finger to his lips.

She heard faint voices approaching from the opposite wing. It sounded like the Earl and a few other men.

Kos pulled his gun. Urgency sped his whispered instructions. "Let's get out of here, because I know a way out of the grounds where we won't be seen. You and Jess follow me."

When Angel met Jess outside, she whispered, "Just follow me. I'll explain later."

Shrubbery and hedges hid them as they rounded the corner. When they had cleared the hedges, Kos stopped and scouted the clearing ahead of them. Minutes later, the three crouched low, running about a hundred yards across an open grassy area. A full moon lit the meadow, increasing the risk.

Panting and gasping, they stopped at a chain link fence hidden by tall hedges. Kos parted the dense hedges and held up a flap of cut chain-link fencing. Jess wiggled through first.

"Hurry, hurry," commanded Kos. Pounding footsteps and shouting men carrying flashlights closed in behind them. Kos hollered, "Run."

Then Angel made a fatal mistake. She looked behind her. Her heart dropped when she saw one of the pursuers had caught Kos in a chokehold. As his captor dragged him backwards, he dug in his heels. Breaking free, Kos spun and landed a powerful punch in the big man's belly. The man dropped the gun and doubled over in pain, but recovered swiftly and retaliated with a hard uppercut to Kos's chin. The man's heavyweight size overpowered the slight frame and lighter weight of Kos, who sagged to the ground, unconscious.

In a matter of seconds, another pursuer grabbed Angel's leg before she crawled under the fence. He caught her and jerked her to her feet. She bit and kicked, but he swore and gave her a hard backhand slap, cutting her lip and bloodying her nose.

The third pursuer, Charles, buzzed the gates open and ran down the road, searching the nearby woods bordering the driveway. He returned empty-handed. He shouted to the others, "The other girl got out." He ran deeper into the woods.

Chapter 25

The Power of Prayer

Jess, shivering, emerged from the woods lining the drive. She was out. She hesitated, watching the figures silhouetted on the castle grounds, one with what looked like a body slung over his shoulder and another dragging a smaller, struggling form.

"Oh God, save them, please. Don't let them get killed," she prayed.

After making certain no one had followed her, she took off running down the graveled road toward the village, praying repeatedly the single prayer she remembered from the Bible. "The Lord is my shepherd; the Lord is my shepherd."

Weakened from drugs and exhaustion, Jess ducked into the thicket bordering the road to rest a little. She sat on a stump, rubbed and blew on her hands, and put them into her jacket pockets. Her right hand struck an object, and with relief, she remembered the cell phone Angel had handed off to her. She keyed in her home number with shaking fingers.

⌘　⌘　⌘

Back in Sugar Land, the neighbors, churches, the community, and the nation had mobilized, searched, supported, and prayed for the Nelsons. Special twenty-four hour prayer vigils were organized throughout the nation; women brought the Nelson family casseroles, cakes, cookies, or simple offers of help where needed. The sophisticated suburban community rallied like a small town.

Law enforcement people at the home-based command center appreciated the unlimited coffee and food. Screening phone calls and visitors fell to the teens, who devised a rotational system. Other teens and children passed out flyers throughout the region.

The Nelsons filled every waking minute with activity until they collapsed into their beds from exhaustion. Their home and serene neighborhood hummed like a busy hive, but always with that sense of expectant hope for good news.

The breakthrough arrived at five o'clock, U.S. time, on the evening of the fourth day. Eric had dished himself a plate of chicken casserole when the phone rang. He rushed and picked it up. Conversations stopped and everyone listened and hoped.

"Hello?" He pushed the speaker button.

Static crackled for a few seconds.

"Hello, hello?"

"Daddy?"

He collapsed in the nearest chair. Agents scurried to phones and computers for a trace on the call. Monica and Anne crowded around him.

"Jess. Jessica, baby, is that you? Are you okay? Where are you?"

"Oh-h-h, Daddy, it's awful ...they took me...prison...forcing drugs into..."

"Jess. You're breaking up. *Where* are you?"

"...Eng–"

Sweat beaded Eric's forehead. He grabbed the receiver, straining to hear. He glanced at the agent on the trace, who shook his head and continued keying into his laptop.

"England? Where in England?" Nothing. Disconnected.

Anne and Monica shed tears of relief, holding each other. The other people applauded and laughed. Anne raised her tear-stained face and opened her arms to Eric. "At least she's alive, Eric."

"I got something." The agent peered into the screen, jotting numbers on a notepad and speaking into the mouthpiece of his headphones.

The family crowded around him, and he held up his hand stopping their anxious questions. "Mm-hm. Check. Okay, good. She's been missing for four or five days. No ransom calls, but the case *is* a kidnapping based on a tip called in by an unidentified informant—yeah, notify the Yard ASAP."

The special agent removed his headphones and addressed the anxious family. "Don't worry. They located the radio tower. She'll be found within a matter of hours."

"Tell us. Where is she? Is she okay? When can we see her?" Eric, Anne, and Monica asked questions all at once.

Palm outward, the agent held up his hand and said, "Hold it. One at a time."

A grin raised the corners of his mouth. "I suggest you pack a few things and prepare to fly to London as soon as you can."

⌘ ⌘ ⌘

Jess tapped and shook the phone but nothing happened. The indicator showed the phone needed re-charging. Hot, salty tears streamed down her cheeks, leaking into the corners of her mouth. Just hearing her father's voice brought an ache. Then, deep sobs racked her body. When she quieted, she heard a voice. No one was around. She looked up, listening.

Like a whisper in her ear she heard, *all is well, my child. I am with you.* Her grief lifted and peace settled over her, and she resumed her search for help.

As she neared the village, she saw a glowing steeple above the trees. Fixing her eyes on the steeple, she came upon a stone church. Ivy clung to its outer walls. Steps led to the well-lit, open doors. She rushed in. No one was in the vestibule. She saw people scattered among the pews, kneeling with heads bowed.

The Power of Prayer

A minister did not stand at the pulpit, nor did an organist play music—just people with bowed heads, praying. As distressed as she was, she couldn't just barge in when people were praying. Looking around, she searched for an office. She must find somebody—fast—and send help to Kos and Angel.

A pair of large brown eyes under a mop of curly dark hair peeped around the sanctuary door. Beside the child, a young woman kneeled, deep in prayer. Jess squatted, making eye contact with the child. The shy little girl placed her thumb in her mouth but she didn't retreat. Jess held out her arms and whispered, "Hi. My name's Jessica; what's yours?" After a little gentle coaxing, the little girl stepped closer.

"Rhoda," she said. The thumb popped back into her mouth.

"Rhoda, will you get your mom and bring her out here?"

The child nodded, went to her mother, and tugged her skirt.

As Jess waited, a hand-printed placard caught her eye. She drew closer and her breath caught in her throat. The sign read, "Welcome to the Prayer Vigil for the American Teen-ager, Jessica." Beneath that, smaller printing read: "Please enter and exit quietly as a courtesy to others still praying."

Awed, Jess fell to her knees, thanking God, and then collapsed in a dead faint.

Chapter 26

Divine Intervention

The heavyset thug dumped Kos's unconscious body on the sofa where the Earl waited in his basement office. The master of the manor wore a hooded, black robe, giving him a diabolic look.

"Not there," he ordered. "Bind his hands and feet securely to that chair over there." He nodded toward an armless oak chair in the corner.

Another man entered, holding Angel, shrieking and clawing.

A pleased smile formed on the Earl's face. "Ahh, it's the vicious little wildcat."

He tossed a coil of heavy rope at the man. "Looks like she must be subdued. Tie her hands and tape up her screeching mouth."

The brute's muscled arm—the same circumference as a sapling—had her in an arm lock. Spent and exhausted, Angel stopped struggling. *My body may be weak, but my mind works just fine.* Strong survival skills spurred her on. Another plan came to her. She must take the Earl by surprise in some way — somehow. *I will not give up without a fight to the death.*

Shoving her into a chair, her captor slapped electrical tape over her mouth and tied her hands around the rear of the chair. He didn't tie her feet; an oversight Angel hoped might cost them. She had strong and flexible legs from years of dancing and training in kickboxing. No one but A.P. and Philomena knew that. She counted on Jess's escape and sending help. The scales almost balanced.

With murder in his eyes, the Earl scowled at each man. He said, "Where's the other girl?"

Inching backward, one answered, "She got outside the fence, your Lordship, but Charles went after her — he should show up any minute now."

"Hmmm. Both of you are fortunate I'm in a good mood, or I'd kill you." He drew a revolver from the desk drawer. "Get out before I change my mind. Keep your mouths closed. It's up to you. I'm sure neither of you want the police involved considering your criminal records. In fact, you may prefer prison. Remember, I'll hunt you down and your death won't be quick."

They ran. The Earl watched, amusement twitching his lips.

He directed his attention to Angel. She didn't flinch or look away, but it crossed her mind that this man had dead eyes — like a killer shark circling his next meal. Once more, she felt evil reaching out from emptiness and darkness through human eyes. The same demonic entity had appeared in Philomena's eyes less than a week ago. She prayed to herself, *this is too powerful— God, send angels–a bolt of lightning–any help. God, you've been so good; don't leave us.*

The Earl broke eye contact first and moved to the desk.

Kos shook his head groggily, regaining consciousness to the unhappy realization that a gag covered his mouth and hands, and that his feet were bound to a chair.

"He's coming to. Very good. I want him fully conscious when I put a bullet in his head," the Earl stated flatly, glancing at her.

Angel's heart squeezed. *God wouldn't actually let him do it, would he?* Hope flickered when he hesitated and dropped his hand to his side.

"On second thought, you both should hear what I have to say before you pass on to–" He smiled at Angel. "–to eternal oblivion."

He placed the gun on the desk and crossed his arms. "Consider this a private press conference. I'm removing the tape from your mouth, wildcat, so you will be free to ask me any questions your feline curiosity may have."

Angel's adrenaline pumped, hoping if she stalled him long enough, the police would make it in time. As long as he had an audience to hear his boasts, he'd keep them alive.

He walked to her. "I'll take this off carefully and slowly so I don't burn your pretty skin."

Like a lover uncovering his beloved's hair, he peeled the heavy tape from her mouth. Tears of pain sprung to Angel's eyes, but she refused to cry out. *He's a psychopathic sadist.* She had sensed that from the beginning.

He seated himself on the sofa, the gun back in his hand and pointed at them. "You might ask why I seek only young, virginal girls. Quite simple, really."

He smiled. "Whatever is offered to *me,* the high priest, must be pure and lovely."

He inclined his head to Angel. "Dear Cousin Arnold, always so cooperative and enterprising, sent you and the other girl—for a good price, I must say."

He hiked up the robe, crossing his legs, adding, "You didn't see the rest of the video—close-ups when the sweet little lambs realize they are going to die. So lovely." He stared dreamily at the wall.

Something inside her chilled to ice. Never had she met a human being so inhuman and narcissistic. Philomena frightened her, but this—this monster was hideous. Little girls. He takes their lives as if they were a piece of meat and then throws them away with the scraps. She had to ask. "Where do these girls come from? Surely not all from A.P."

"Ah yes, I thought you'd ask that question. That's where my spiritual master has arranged matters in my favor." With deliberate irony, he shaped his fingers into a steeple.

After a moment he said, "I own all the land in this area, which includes the village. It's part of my inheritance. It just so happens there's a small orphanage at the edge of the village, built and funded by my family. Some key people there honor my spiritual position and bring their offerings, carefully selected beforehand. Therefore, from time to time girls disappear—and, of course, because they are orphans there is no family—"

Sharp raps on the door interrupted.

"Go away until I send for you."

The raps escalated into pounding.

"Your Lordship," he shouted, "It's Charles. We have to get out. The police are coming."

The Earl jerked the door open. "Where's the other girl?"

Charles's eyes flicked to the gun in his hand. The butler's normally composed expression twisted in fear. He stammered, "S-sir, she escaped. I-I searched thoroughly, but—"

"—You idiot. I put you in charge of security. Now, one of them is completely off the property. I do not tolerate *shoddy* work."

He waved the gun in Charles's face. "Well, we must deal with that. Move over with the girl and the man."

Charles edged into the hall, but the Earl placed the cocked gun on the butler's chest, the muzzle pressed tight against his left ribcage. Without moving the gun, the Earl guided Charles inside and kicked the door shut. Pushing him toward Angel and Kos, he kept the gun trained on him. "Just as I thought. I cannot trust anyone—not even you, Charles—so I have no choice. I cannot let you go free; you know too much. I must destroy *everything* that can be used as evidence against me."

He sidestepped to the safe, gathering papers and videocassettes with one hand, keeping the gun pointed at them with the other, and tossed the records into the blazing fire. He didn't take his eyes off any of his captives. When he was done, he picked up a can of gasoline and doused the drapes, the floor, and the furniture.

Angel's heart stopped. *He's going to burn us alive.* She wiggled and rubbed her bound wrists against the arm of the chair. She looked desperately at Kos. He bucked and heaved trying to free himself from his bonds. Charles, although unbound, didn't move and kept his eyes wide and fixed on the gun in the Earl's hand. "Please, please don't kill me," he begged.

Ignoring him, the Earl said, "Charles, I need some insurance in the event I encounter the police. Bring the girl to me. Move, idiot."

Angel felt more panic rise inside her, but she stayed quiet as Charles loosened her hands, grasped her shoulders, and pushed her toward the Earl. When she came closer, she thought she detected panic in the Earl's eyes. He pulled her tightly to his body, tossing a lit match into the pooling fluid beneath the heavy draperies lining the wall behind Kos and Charles. Flames flared up the draperies and crept to the puddles of gasoline. Angel struggled, making it difficult for the Earl to back toward the door.

Charles, with a change of heart, rushed to Kos and untied him, but the fire snaked closer, blocking them with thick smoke and leaping flames.

Angel coughed and choked, and her body sagged, forcing the Earl to drag her. Pulling the cowl of his robe over his face to block the smoke, the slightly built Earl had difficulty handling Angel's dead weight. They were almost to the outer door. He loosened his grip when he tripped on the hem of his robe and fell. Angel escaped when he released her as he went down. The gun went off and the bullet lodged harmlessly in the ceiling.

In horror, she watched the flames creep from the hem of his robe, setting him aflame in seconds. Blood-curdling screams came from the Earl as he writhed and rolled in agony. The screams stopped. His body jerked a few times and stilled as the flames consumed it.

"Kos. Charles. Where are you," Angel screamed over the roar of the flames.

She squatted, thrust her hands into a nearby pool of flames, and burned the rope free, suffering serious burns on her wrists and hands. Ignoring her injuries, she pulled out her shirttail with her unbound hands and covered her mouth with the cloth.

"Over here." Kos's shout drifted through the smoke.

"Follow the sound of my voice—I'm by the door."

The fire roared all about the room, and she dropped to the floor, repeating her shouts between choking coughs.

She made out two crawling figures emerging from the curtain of smoke. The three, despite the intense heat of the heavy metal door, pushed it open, and tumbled into the hallway.

"Run–it's spreading to the basement and when it reaches the gas furnace it's gonna blow," shouted Kos.

When the last one reached the top step of the basement, an explosion propelled them across the floor. Scrambling outside, they ran beyond the gardens toward the gates.

From a safe distance, they heard more booms and saw the fire working its way through the east wing.

Kos restrained Charles and pulled his gun.

Angel's mouth dropped.

Kos shrugged and said, "I got lucky. They never searched me."

A coughing fit grabbed him, but between coughs, he told Charles, "FBI—you are under—arrest for conspiracy in the—the kidnapping of Angela Ross and Jessica Nelson. You have the right to remain silent…."

She hadn't a clue that Kos was FBI. He had a lot of explaining to do.

Chapter 27

Moving On

The full moon shone on the turreted tower silhouettes of the seven-hundred year-old fortress. Behind the towers huddled a thick grove of trees, spreading to the rolling hills of the English countryside. Only crickets' songs broke the silence.

An explosion shattered the rural peace, and black smoke mushroomed from the east wing. Like ants, figures emerged from the grove fanning the crest of the nearest hill and disappeared into the valleys and hollows beyond. A solitary figure paused at the crest of a hill.

Philomena, dressed in her native ceremonial clothing, stared at the flames licking the castle, muttering, "That will teach that fool he don't mess around with the power of Philomena's curses."

She threw back her head, laughing deep from her belly, and walked toward the village.

⌘   ⌘   ⌘

Above the clamor of sirens, smaller explosions, and police radios, Angel shouted to the ambulance attendant she was okay and didn't need to go to the hospital, even though it hurt her throat just to speak.

"Only my hands are burned a little, and I can—"

"—Pardon me, miss."

A man approached her, removing his derby. Taking his wallet from inside his jacket, he opened it and showed it to her. "I'm Detective Thomas Smythe with Scotland Yard." The attendant stepped back after Smythe spoke a few words to him. The detective then led her to a small sedan parked on the grass. Stepping aside and holding the door on the passenger side, he gestured her inside.

The detective entered on the driver's side, closing the door behind him. He turned to her and said, "There. Now we are out of the dreadful din so we can talk a few moments and sort things out. You are aware, of course, that as soon as possible I must ask you a few questions. However, may I persuade you that a comfortable hospital room, private and secluded, is more suitable than here or our musty old offices at headquarters? Your injuries must be treated first."

Away from the noise and distractions, the sting of pain in her hands increased and the burning in her lungs and esophagus made inhaling painful. Yes, she supposed she was better off in the hospital, but her true desire was a hideaway where she could decide what to do with the rest of her life. She couldn't bear to face people right now.

She spoke, but with difficulty over the hoarseness. "I guess so, but I have some questions of my own. What happened to Jessica? Did you catch A.P.? Philomena?"

"Hold on, Miss Ross. Your injuries are worse than you may realize and you need treatment and rest, so wouldn't it be better for you to go along to the hospital? Time enough for answering your questions later, and for you to answer ours."

"But—"

Smythe stepped out of the car. Exhausted, and unable to hold her body upright, Angel slumped against the door. Detective Smythe beckoned the ambulance attendant before opening her door and assisting her.

While the stretcher passed Smythe, he tipped his hat to Angel. "A pleasure to meet you, Miss Ross. I'll check on you later. Good evening."

⌘ ⌘ ⌘

The bus depot in the village had a few passengers waiting for the last bus to London. Most were working class men on their annual journey to the city looking for work through the winter. A drowsy clerk sat on a stool behind a window with a sign above it, reading, "Purchase Tickets Here."

Philomena walked to the ticket counter and purchased her ticket, looking neither right nor left. She knew her exotic attire drew stares, but she was proud of her calling. She sat on a bench facing the plate glass window overlooking the main street of the village. She folded her hands and placed them into her lap, serene and calm. Darkened, closed shops lined the cobblestone street. She was lost in her private visions; nevertheless, her sharp eyes detected movement in the shadows beyond the rectangle of light cast onto the sidewalk.

A slender figure emerged, approaching the depot entry with hesitant steps. She clutched a coin purse to her chest. She stopped outside the door, straightening her shoulders as if for courage, and entered.

Philomena watched the girl, who looked young — about twelve or thirteen. She wore an old-fashioned print dress much too big for her and a headscarf. A few dark curls peeped from beneath the scarf. The men watched her, too, and she backed to the door when a few of the young ones greeted her with whistles and catcalls.

Philomena stood, rising to her full height, and directed a malevolent stare at the men, silencing them. They moved away. She approached the girl, took her hand like a child, and walked to the ticket counter with her.

"Now, child, you be with me and I won' let nobody hurt you."

The frightened girl opened her coin purse and purchased her ticket while Philomena stared down the leering men again and led the girl to a bench in the back of the depot.

"Now, tell ole Philomena what you doin' here without your mama and daddy."

The girl hung her head and replied, "Have no ma or da', Ma'am."

"Oh my, my, my." Philomena clucked like a mother hen. "What's your name, child?"

The girl bowed her head, peeking sideways at her. "You won't call the sheriff, will you," she asked in a trembling voice.

Philomena straightened, turning the girl's chin around for eye contact. "Who you runnin' away from—where have you come from?"

Philomena coaxed the frightened girl into disclosing her name and dilemma. Fiona had run away from the orphanage outside the village after her best friend disappeared. Rumors started—awful rumors—about selling orphan kids to bad people for sex or as slaves.

Philomena comforted and held the girl until the arrival of the bus. Above the roar and wheezing of the bus, she said, "I have an idea."

Fiona raised her tear-stained face, and Philomena found a handkerchief in her bag, wiped away the tears, and continued, "You stay with me and I'll find you a good, safe home after we get to London."

Fiona nodded, and looked relieved. Philomena drew the child's face to her breast, patting her head with tenderness. As she stared over her head, a smile tipped the corners of her mouth and a gleam lit her dark eyes.

Philomena's thoughts, always hidden from everyone, were not charitable or compassionate for the girl. A.P. and his cousin had stolen Angel from her—someone she had groomed and trained for years for a higher calling—for their own greedy purposes. Their treachery had brought their own bad end, but she had escaped and it's time for her to return to her village. The spirits called her, and she would not return empty-handed.

Chapter 28

A Family Reunited

As soon as the Nelsons arrived in London, the news media crowded around them, shouted questions, and held out microphones. Anne and Monica, their heads down and faces turned away from the cameras, hurried through the throng of reporters.

Eric paused in front of a microphone and said, "We're overjoyed our daughter is alive, but we have no more information at this time. The FBI is handling everything and the investigation is still open. Now, please let us by so we can see our daughter."

Airport Security and the FBI special agent escorting the family dispersed the reporters and onlookers and the family moved on.

Monica felt the chill and dampness the moment the family stepped outside the airport. They had left Houston in a hurry; there wasn't time for simple matters like packing warmer clothes.

After everyone settled inside the comfortable limousine, the FBI agent said, "Now that it's quieter, let me introduce myself. I'm Ken White, Special Agent in Charge, London Field Office."

He presented his badge. Eric glanced at it and nodded. "Yes, we believe you, Agent White; it's not necessary to examine your credentials." He leaned forward, searched White's eyes, and said, "Is there any more news? Is Jessica all right?"

White relaxed against the back of the seat and extracted a small notebook from his inside pocket. Glancing at it, he said, "This is what we know at this time. She ran to a church in Wortham Village, looking disheveled and very frightened, and collapsed when the Vicar arrived. He called an ambulance, which transported her to–" He flipped a few pages until he found the name and address. "– Kent County Hospital in Sevenoaks, a town about an hour's drive from here. We're taking you there now."

Several hours later, Monica hesitated at the door of Jess's room, frightened and unsure of what she should say. Oh, she felt glad about her sister—that she was alive—but after the doctor told them about her mind and gave the family warnings about how they should behave, she didn't know what to do. She didn't know anything about mental illness, but she couldn't imagine her lovable, hateful, admirable, and disgusting sister any other way.

God, I don't understand about post-traumatic stress, amnesia, or any of the names the doctor said, but you do. I'm so sorry about the mean ways I treated her and looked down on her, but you know I love her. Will she remember those things? Will she remember me? Help, help, please.

With another quick prayer for courage, Monica pushed the door open. Icy with shock, she stared at the figure in the bed. She thought at first she was in the wrong room.

Jess was thin, and her collarbones stuck out above the faded blue hospital gown. Freckles stood out on her pale face and sunken cheeks. Her limp, dull hair hung to her shoulders.

"Monica?" Jess's voice quivered.

Monica's heart broke. She couldn't imagine God being so cruel. Jess's eyes were wide and the pupils dilated, as if in a perpetual state of fear.

"Yes, Jess, it's me." She wanted to take Jess in her arms and hold her like a baby. Approaching her, she opened her arms to give her a hug, but Jessica's eyes widened and she shrank back in the pillows.

Monica dropped her arms, dumbstruck. What was this? She couldn't even touch her own twin sister. She backed away and stood at the foot of the bed.

Jess's tension relaxed, but an anxious expression stayed on her face. "Where am I, Monica. Why am I in the hospital? I feel all right. Did I miss the party?"

"Party," asked Monica. "What party?"

"Our birthday party, of course."

Monica said gently, "That happened a month ago, Jess. Don't you remember?"

Jessica didn't answer and her eyes sunk back into their sockets, haunted and drained of life.

All of a sudden, in a shocking mood change, Jess struggled out of bed and charged straight for Monica, burning hatred in her eyes.

She screamed, "Go away. Stop torturing me."

A nurse dashed in and wrestled Jessica back to the bed and pinned her down; another followed with a syringe in her hand.

Monica ran from the room, sobbing, straight into the arms of her mother.

⌘　⌘　⌘

That night, after the family had dinner in the hotel restaurant, Monica dropped to her knees by the bed. *God, I don't understand. What happened to my sister's mind? Was it so horrible she'll never get her memory back? Lord, please bring the real Jessica back; heal her. What do you want me to do for her?*

Before she went to sleep, she knew the answer. A long struggle lay ahead, but she made a promise to take care of Jess the rest of her life, if necessary.

Chapter 29

Aftermath and a Visitor

Two weeks later, Kos arrived in Houston. After placing Charles into the custody of British authorities, he checked in with the FBI field office in London, after which he flew to FBI Headquarters in Washington, D.C., for medical evaluation and interviews. Because he had *unofficially* continued undercover, he received an informal reprimand, but thankfully, they released him for a new assignment from his home base.

Throughout the entire tedious process, Kos privately contacted the hospital in London for updates on Angel's condition. His last check revealed her condition had improved enough for transport by air ambulance to Houston's Medical Center.

He paid her a visit as soon as he arrived in Houston. The extreme concern he had for this woman took him by surprise, but he would keep his emotions under control.

However, Kos barely recognized Angel when he entered the room. The beautiful, vibrant star looked like a lost child. Dark smudges bruised the skin beneath her eyes. Her body was fragile and thin and he wanted to pick her up and hold her.

He ignored the tender feelings that welled up. He told himself, *Be friendly, but distant.*

"At last. The heroine can have visitors," he joked.

Her cheerless smile reminded him the situation was no joking matter.

He seated himself in the chair across from her, bent forward, and rested his hands on his knees.

Angel drew the blanket tighter around her, drawing her legs under her.

"Did Jess get away? Is she okay?"

"Yes to both questions. As we speak she is home with her family."

Kos hesitated, and then said, "Before I go any further, I guess I owe you some explanations."

Plunging on, he said, "I am a special agent with the FBI and formerly on the team of an international task force formed for finding organizations or people involved with trafficking children and teens for sex or slavery."

Angel looked at him in genuine surprise. Shuddering, she said, "Children? Slavery? No, no, A.P. wouldn't do that, would he?" She buried her face in her hands, her words muffled. "Oh-o-o. I'm so ashamed I went along with such a scheme even for a little while, but-but I didn't know everything."

"We know that, Angel. We put bugs in Peck's office and your hotel suite, so we have recorded evidence. We found a duplicate set of books, which show he embezzled most of your money in the trust fund. The IRS wants him, too."

Angel took her hands from her face, paying close attention to each disclosure of A.P.'s crimes. Then she said something surprising to Kos.

"I think Philomena is in trouble with the IRS, too, and I found out a few years ago she sold drugs out of her home."

Kos chose his words carefully. "Uh-oh. This puts another wrinkle in the case. Dependent upon the laws of Texas, if you knew about the drug trafficking and didn't report it to the police, you may be viewed as a co-conspirator to a felony."

Alarmed, Angel said, "But I was only thirteen at the time and under her guardianship. Surely they wouldn't prosecute a child guilty of that."

"Look, don't get upset. Philomena has much bigger matters—federal crimes—to deal with first."

Angel relaxed.

Kos continued, "I don't think Philomena knew about the embezzlement, but we have evidence she's a co-conspirator in the kidnapping plot. In addition, some investigative work by our office in London came up with information she's had connections with a satanic cult, which we found located on Beckingham's estate. She's practiced witchcraft for years."

"Uh—I've known about that, too, but I was very afraid of her; I'm afraid of her now, too."

Before she could go any further, Angel's face paled, and she clutched at her throat.

"Look—you're in pain. We can talk about the rest another time."

She shook her head and choked out, "No, go on. I'm fine."

He shot a sharp look at her, but continued. "I turned over the incriminating tapes and documents I took from Beckingham's safe to the local authorities."

"Wait—you keep mentioning someone named Beckingham. Who's Beckingham?" Before Kos answered, Angel started coughing again, putting her in danger of collapsing.

Kos charged toward the door for help, but Angel recovered her breath and stopped him.

"No," she gasped. "Just–help–me–to the–bed." Between words, she took a breath from an inhaler she had pulled out of her pocket.

Kos lifted her from the chair, touched that she weighed so little. While she rested, Kos reconsidered telling her more. He doubted she could withstand testifying at the trial if it came up too soon. He'd need clearance, but the government may place her in the Witness Protection Program until the trial.

Angel stirred, rearranged her pillows, and raised the head of the hospital bed. She breathed normally and could speak, but barely above a whisper. She said, "You were telling me about this Beckingham person. Who is he?"

"Beckingham is the Earl's legal surname. It seems his family requested nondisclosure of his title to divert a scandal to the family name. Few knew his surname. Since he is dead and left no heirs, his property reverts to the Crown."

Angel nodded. "Go on."

"Scotland Yard is pretty far along with their investigation about missing children from the orphanage located on his property. They've rounded up the administrator and staff for questioning about alleged murders of some missing children. Someone erased each missing child's records and didn't notify the law."

"You mean the children I saw on the videotape were killed?"

"Yes. We viewed all of the tapes, and the ritual you saw culminated with–er–the death of the children."

Angel leaned back into the pillows and closed her eyes.

"What about Philomena?"

"She escaped, and to the best of our knowledge, hasn't returned to the States. We seized the contents of your hotel suite and her residence in Houston. She was last seen two weeks ago boarding a bus from the village to London."

She sighed. "The doctors said I won't recover my singing voice because of this." She touched her throat.

After a long pause, she said, "I knew that my concerts weren't drawing the audiences we needed. That's my fault." Spots of color reddened her pale cheeks and she stammered, "I was drinking too much because I hated my life. Between the drugs Philomena fed me and the drinking, my performances were dismal. I knew my career was sliding downhill. I tried to run away, but A.P.'s hired thugs grabbed me."

"I know."

"What about A.P.?"

"I was getting to him. Peck had been under suspicion for a long time for suspected trafficking activities, and that's why I went undercover."

For a moment, a mischievous gleam returned the sparkle to her eyes. She grinned and said, "You were good. You sure had me fooled. Where did you learn to dance like that? I wouldn't think Quantico trained you for it."

His neck flushed, and he ran his finger around his collar.

"Uh—it just happens that I was a dancer in Romania before I came on board with the FBI."

"Oh, a man of mystery. It wouldn't just happen that you have a Gypsy background," she teased.

He shifted uncomfortably. Even from a hospital bed, she was seductive, and he had difficulty keeping his mind on business. Angel had had that effect on him since he first met her.

Kos changed the subject. "I have to tell you something that may not please you, but it's necessary. We have arrested Peck, but his lawyer probably will get him out on bond. Also, we haven't arrested the ringleaders of the trafficking organization. They liquidated his talent business. Your assets, which he controls and which are left, must be frozen until the outcome of his trial. We've uprooted a tightly knit and extensive operation. You're a material witness."

"I'm willing to testify."

"There is a problem. Until it's over and all the bad guys are in prison, you're in a high level of danger. Any attempts you make to touch the money in your trust, which you need to live on, will put you in peril and hinder our investigation."

Kos searched her eyes. "Philomena imposes a threat, too, until we locate her. So, those are the reasons we must give you a new identity and place you in the Witness Protection Program. I just have to clear it with my superiors. You going to be okay with that?"

Shaking, Angel dropped back on the pillows and closed her eyes. "Do whatever you wish. Now if you don't mind, I need to rest for awhile."

⌘　⌘　⌘

After he left, she thought, *I'd be a prisoner all over again. Oh, God, when will I get a life? When will I ever stop feeling lonely?*

Such thoughts plagued her the rest of the afternoon. That evening after dinner, she tried reading, ignoring the laughter and greetings of the visitors and families of other patients on her floor. After awhile, she put down her book and turned on the TV, raising the volume as far as she dared so she could drown out the laughter and friendly voices from the other rooms.

A nurse opened her door and peered in. "Miss, are you expecting any visitors? There's a woman insisting on seeing you, but refuses to tell us her full name so we can check if she has clearance. All she says is, 'Tell her it's Darla; she'll know.'"

Elation bloomed in her heart. Lifting her eyes to the ceiling, she murmured, "Thank you, God. You knew all along what I needed."

"Pardon?" The nurse waited for an answer.

"Yes, send her in."

Nine years. Darla always showed up in her life when she needed a friend the most.

Chapter 30

Reunion

"Angela. Are you going to be all right? I'm so glad I found you. I've been looking for you for *years*."

Darla had changed. Her red hair had softened to mahogany with hints of gray at her temples. Her dear, sweet face had lines, and she looked older than a thirty-two-old woman should look. What had happened?

The women hugged each other for several minutes, the reunion too moving for words.

Angel drew away first, smiling through her tears. "It's been so long since anyone has called me by my real name."

Darla tilted her head, a question forming on her lips—

"You don't know?"

"Know what? That's your name, isn't it? That's how I found you–by your name, Angela Ross. The newspaper put that name under your picture. Oh, your hair was different and you were older, but I knew it was you, all right," said Darla.

Angel laughed. "So much for fame. I believed I was so hot and adored by my fans that I assumed *everyone* recognized me."

"You probably were—or are. You see, I don't know anything about celebrities on TV or movies, because I've—" Darla hesitated a few seconds. "— been away."

Darla removed her jacket and placed her handbag on the floor beside her. "Before we go any further, I think you'd better explain how bad your injuries are and what the doctors tell you to expect."

Angel told her about the fire and the extent of her injuries. "So, don't get alarmed if my coughing gets out of control. A brief rest from speaking and a few puffs from my inhaler fix me up."

"How long will this last," asked Darla.

"I don't know. The doctors won't say much. Anyhow, why don't you tell me everything about you?"

Angel looked down at her fidgeting hands. "You know, it hurt a lot when you left No Name without saying goodbye. One day you were—just gone. I haven't forgotten what you taught me about God and Jesus. It got me through a lot."

Angel's mind flew back to that horrible August night when she ran away. She had to talk about it—all of it. She trusted Darla. She began, "You know Pa is dead, don't you?"

Darla didn't react as Angel expected. Instead, her friend picked up her hands and said in a gentle voice, "No, Angela, he didn't die. He was still alive when you ran away."

"What?"

"I discovered him just minutes after you ran away and he was still breathing. The ambulance and the police weren't far behind, and I said nothing about you. None of the people in town said anything about what went on in that shack year after year. A few knew, but the police didn't ask and those few didn't volunteer the information. That must explain why the police didn't look for you."

Angel leaned back and closed her eyes, feeling the blood ebb from her face.

Darla released her hands and moved to the head of the bed, worry written on her face. "Oh, my dear, I didn't realize how weakened your accident left you—I can return tomorrow."

She shook her head. A few minutes later, the shock receded.

Darla returned to her chair, making herself comfortable. "It's a long story, Angela, and not very pretty. Are you up to it?"

"I'm fine," Angel whispered. "Go on."

Nevertheless, unbidden, the old fear of Pa returned. She took a deep, painful breath and added, "Tell me everything—where's Pa now?"

"He'll never hurt you again. He's dead now, but not by your hands."

"How?"

"His wounds from the shooting were severe, and he had significant brain damage, complicated by a stroke while he recovered in the hospital. The stroke increased the brain damage, but when he regained consciousness, many other complications developed.

"What do you mean?"

"I think they said he developed severe aphasia—a condition that causes the loss of power to speak and understand words. He refused rehabilitation, so they transferred him to a skilled nursing facility operated by the State. I heard he died there a few months later."

Angel didn't feel any grief, although she knew she should. The emotion she felt was relief. She was glad he was dead, and she could never forgive him for his cruelty for years—and the final outrage, attempted rape. She must tell Darla *why* she shot him that night. The secret was unbearable.

However, she looked over at Darla, ready to spill out details of that last night at home, but halted when she saw her staring into the distance lost in her own thoughts, tears tracing a steady path down her cheeks.

"Darla—what's the matter?" Angel attempted sitting and getting off the bed so she could comfort Darla. However, her legs wouldn't support her.

"No, no—I'm fine. I'm just broken-hearted that your father—that anyone—is alone and neglected when he dies." Her words trailed off.

"If he had been beating you for years, you wouldn't care if he died alone. He was a mean drunk and nobody liked him.

He brought it on himself," said Angel. Resentment peppered her words.

"Angela, you don't mean that. He was your *father*; he brought you up, fed you and kept a roof over your head ever since your mother—"

"Yeah. What about my mother? Every time I asked, he'd get mad, go out and get drunk, and come home and beat me up. What kind of a father is that?"

It all came back—the nightmares, the wondering, and the loneliness. Rage exploded from the depths of her soul and she wanted to scream out her pain. However, she could do nothing but sob, her injured throat cutting off the screams. The futility of it all washed over her. Hope had died in her, like an unborn child in a mother's womb. She buried her face in the pillows.

Darla waited until Angel was ready and listening.

"I'm sorry, Darla. I'm not mad at you. You came and made it bearable for a few years, longer than I expected. I've never thanked you. If it hadn't been for you I wouldn't have gone to school nor had a God to believe in."

"Don't thank me, my dear child. God had his hand in both our lives all along, and prepared us for the hardships that were ahead."

Angel accepted the tissue Darla handed her. "What do you mean?"

"I haven't told you everything you need to know yet. Your mother's name was Denise and she was my big sister. She ran away from home to marry your father when she knew she was pregnant. None of us heard from her for five years."

Spellbound, Angel heard for the first time about her mother. So, she didn't abandon her, and the fragments of memories began to reassemble and make sense.

The minutes grew to an hour before Darla concluded.

"Attention everyone. Visiting hours are over. All visitors must leave now.
Thank you."

"Don't go yet," Angel pleaded. "It's okay if you stay a little longer. "You didn't explain how you found Pa and what happened to you after that."

Darla recounted the details of that night, ending, "And so, they took me into custody for attempted murder because I was standing over the body when they arrived. That night while I sat in prison, I prayed—not for God to help *me* but to protect *you*."

She continued, "I figured he had beat you one time too many and you shot him in self-defense, and while I was on my knees on that cold floor in the cell, God sent me a clear-cut plan. It didn't sound right at first, but the prompting wouldn't go away. So, I confessed to the Sheriff, claiming revenge as a motive.

I wanted to keep you out of it. The investigation and judicial process took about a year, and I stayed in jail until they brought me before the Judge—"

"Oh, no. You did that for me? Oh, Darla."

"But, you see, that was God's plan all along. Many of those women in jail were lost and needing a Savior and the Lord had prepared me and equipped me already. The Judge reduced the charge from attempted murder to aggravated assault; he sentenced me to a year, and then released me for time already served. Many prisoners had turned their lives around. When I got out, I knew that God had a prison ministry set out as my work for Him."

"You're so strong, Darla. Even though we were apart, because of you, I turned to God for help and He was always there. For a long time, I was so lost and caught up in evil, but God delivered me. I'll never turn away again."

"That's why I knew God had a hand in this when I saw that newspaper article, asked a few questions, and found you. It's time to get on with the rest of God's mission."

"There's more?"

"Much more. You see, I've raised money to buy land and build a camp for lost young girls—a place where they have a home, people who love them, a chance to learn that God loves them, too, and wants them to redirect their lives when they get out of prison."

Darla went on, "I have a proposal for you when you get out of the hospital. How would you like to partner with me in the camp?"

Angel's heart leaped at the offer, but recalling her conversation with Kos crushed her excitement. She said, "I would like that more than anything in the world. I already know my injuries prevent me from singing professionally, which is my first love, but helping girls in trouble gives me another passion."

. "Wonderful. I'll get things started right away—"

"Wait–I can't do it right now. Until the trials are over, according to the FBI I'm in danger because two people and an entire ring of child sex traffickers place me in enough danger that I have to change my identity, address, and my appearance and hide in the Witness Protection Program. Nobody knows how long that will be."

Darla thought that over, then said, "God knows, so I don't have to know how long, just have faith—you, too." She smiled. "I'll save a place for you, regardless of how long it takes."

⌘   ⌘   ⌘

After they had said their goodbyes and Darla left, Angel rested back into the pillows, thinking about the amazing afternoon and evening. Life was wonderful again. It had been such a long time. As everything quieted, she noticed the laughter and greetings from other patients' rooms. This time, it reminded her that she had a family after all, and when a family waited for her, she'd get through this business of the Witness Protection Program. After all, her heart wouldn't change. They could change her and hide her all they wanted, but, inside, she'd still be the person God created her to be.

RESOURCES

Books

- *The Kingdom of Cults,* revised edition, by Dr. Walter Martin (Bethany House, October 2003)
- *Occult Invasion* by Dave Hunt (Harvest House, 1998)
- *Witchcraft Goes Mainstream* by Brooks Alexander (Harvest House, 2004)
- *Jay's Journal* edited by Dr. Beatrice Sparks (Pocket Books, a division of Simon & Schuster, 1979)
- *Good News About Injustice* by Gary A Haugen, president of International Justice Mission in Washington, D.C. (InterVarsity Press, 1999)
- *Spellbound* by Marcia Montenegro (Cook Communications Ministries, 2006)
- *The Holy Bible (NIV)*

<u>Web Site Articles</u>

- *Naworth Castle,* http://www.castleuk.net
- *Development of the English Castle, Part 2,* http://www.britannia.com
- *Dover Castle,* http://www.castlexplorer.co.uk
- *Castle Medieval Tunnels,* http://www.castles-of-britain.com

Made in the USA